I Can Read Comics

introduces children to the world of graphic novel storytelling and encourages visual literacy in emerging readers. Comics inspire reader engagement unlike any other format. They ask readers to infer and answer questions, like:

1. What do I read first? Image or text?
2. Why is this word balloon shaped this way, and that word balloon shaped that way?
3. Why is a character making that facial expression? Are they happy, angry, excited, sad?

From the comics your child reads with you to the first comic they read on their own, there are **I Can Read Comics** for every stage of reading:

LEVEL 1

Simple stories for shared reading.

LEVEL 2

Engaging stories for children reading on their own.

LEVEL 3

Complex stories for independent readers.

The magic of graphic novel storytelling lies between the gutters.
Unlock the magic with…

I Can Read Comics!

Visit **ICanRead.com** for information on enriching your child's reading experience.

I Can Read *Comics* Cartooning Basics

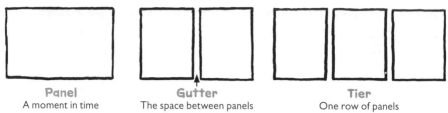

Panel
A moment in time

Gutter
The space between panels

Tier
One row of panels

Word Balloons   When someone talks, thinks, whispers, or screams, their words go in here:

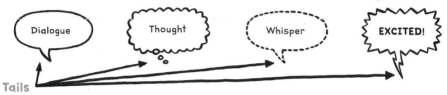

Dialogue

Thought

Whisper

EXCITED!

Tails
Point to whoever is talking / thinking / whispering / screaming / etc.

A quick how-to-read comics guide:

In a **panel**, read the text on the **left** first.

Then, read the text on the **right.**

Remember to...
Read the text along with the image, paying close attention to the character's acting, the action, and/or the scene. Every little detail matters!

No dialogue? No problem!
If there is no dialogue within a panel, take the time to read the image. Visual cues are just as important as text, so don't forget about them!

On a page, **start here**, in the **top left** corner!

After that, read the panel immediately to the **right.**

When you're done up there, come down here and read **this** panel **next!**

ME NEXT! ME NEXT!

You're almost there...

YOU MADE IT! You just read a comic page!

YAY!

To Teddy —S.R.

HarperAlley is an imprint of HarperCollins Publishers.
I Can Read® and I Can Read Book® are trademarks of HarperCollins Publishers.

Fish and Wave
Copyright © 2022 by Sergio Ruzzier
All rights reserved. Printed in the United States of America.
No part of this book may be used or reproduced in any manner whatsoever without written permission except in the case of brief quotations embodied in critical articles and reviews. For information address HarperCollins Children's Books, a division of HarperCollins Publishers, 195 Broadway, New York, NY 10007.
www.icanread.com

Library of Congress Control Number: 2021951491
ISBN 978-0-06-307667-9 (hardcover) — ISBN 978-0-06-307666-2 (pbk.)

Book design by Joe Merkel
22 23 24 25 26   LSCC   10 9 8 7 6 5 4 3 2 1   ❖   First Edition

I Can Read!
Comics

FISH and WAVE

by Sergio Ruzzier

HARPER
alley

An Imprint of HarperCollinsPublishers

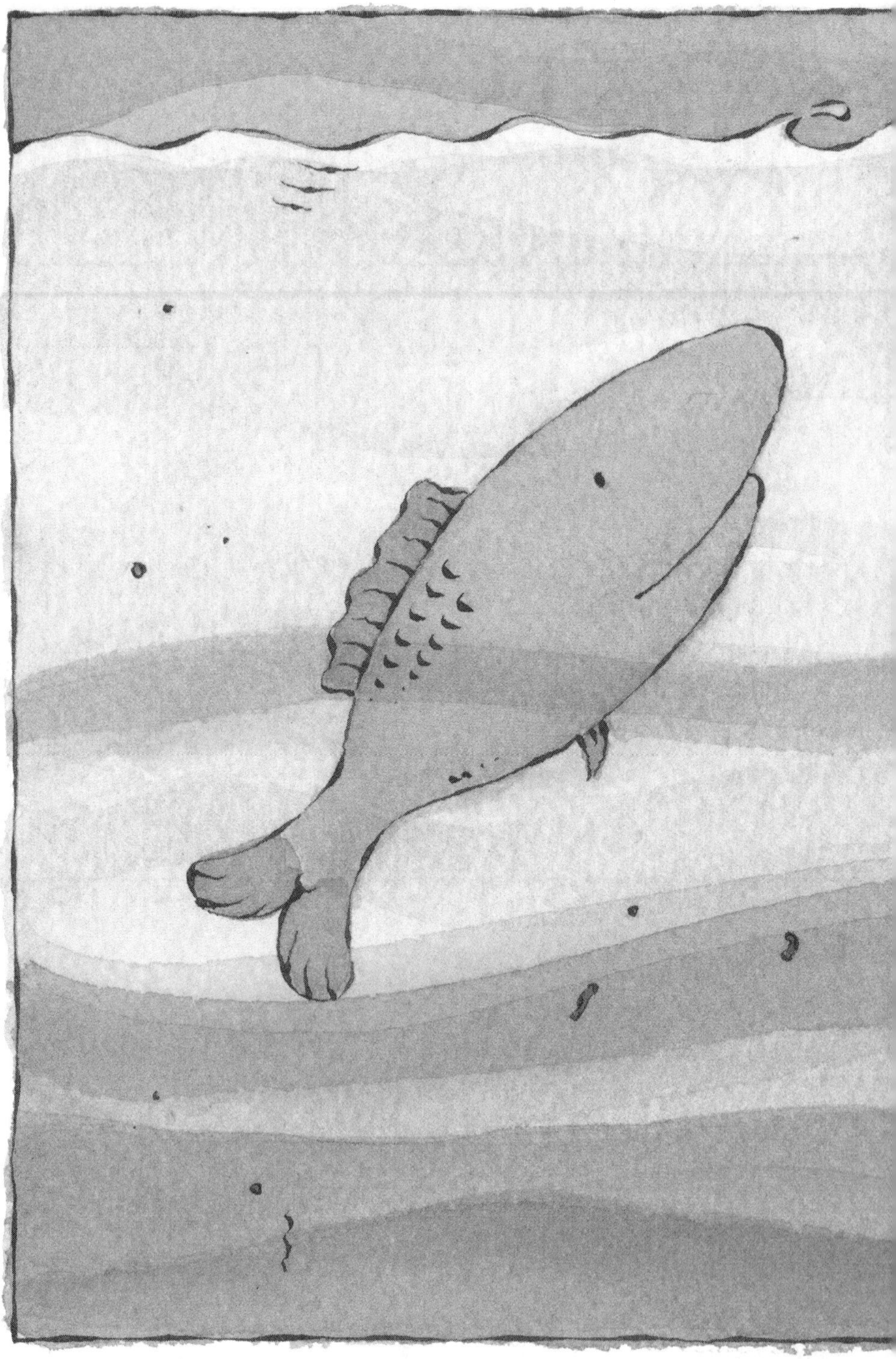

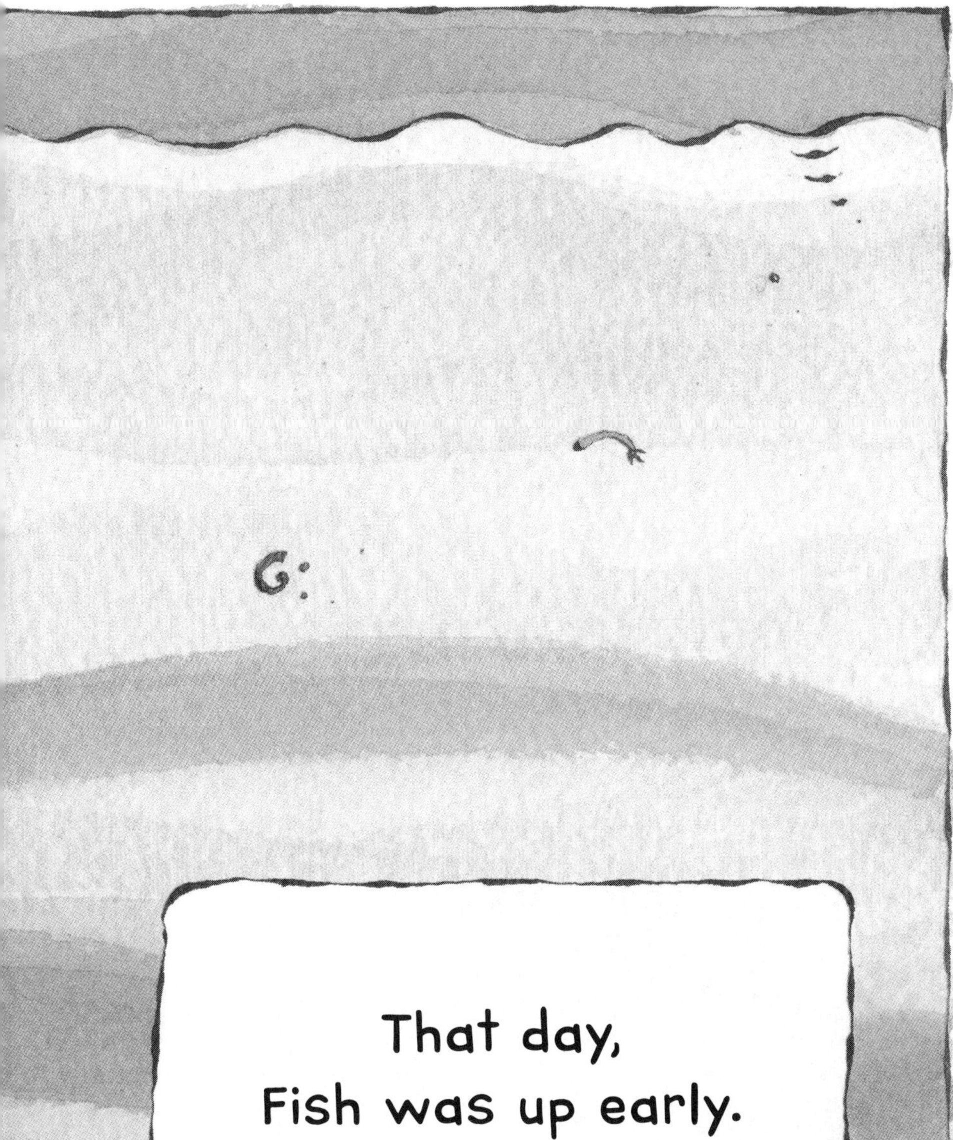

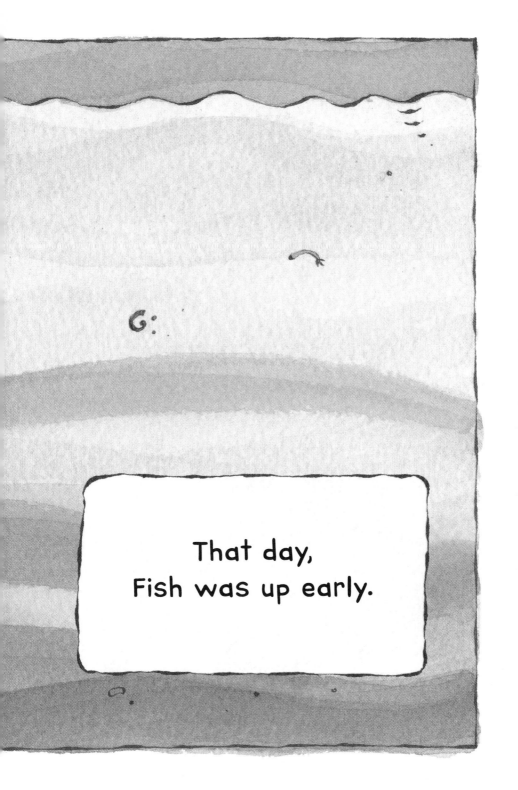

That day,
Fish was up early.

He was looking
for a friend
to play with.

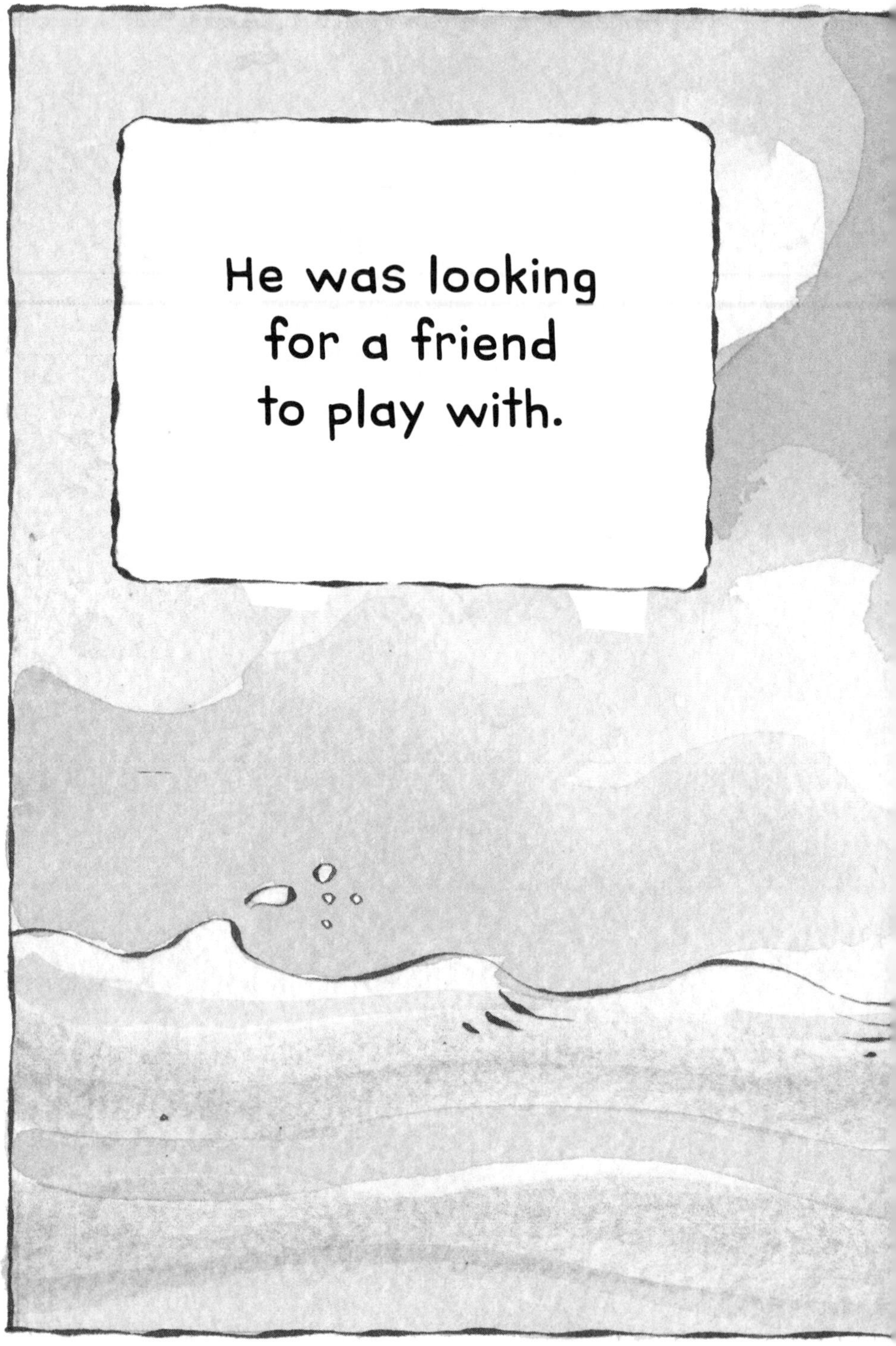

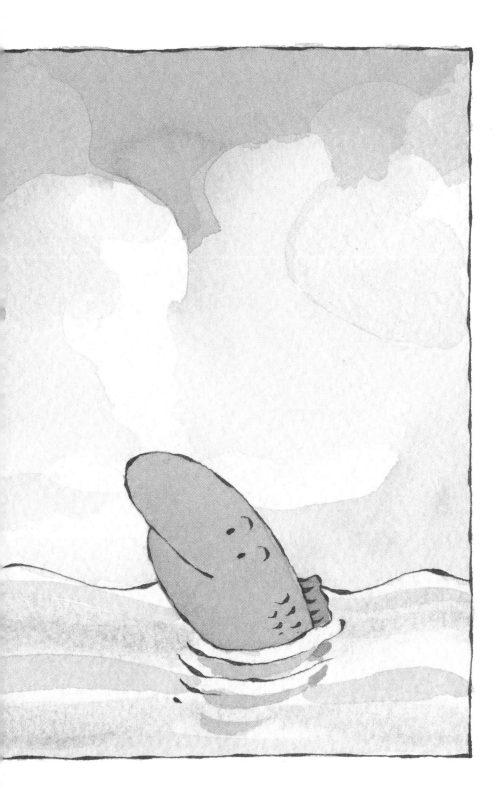

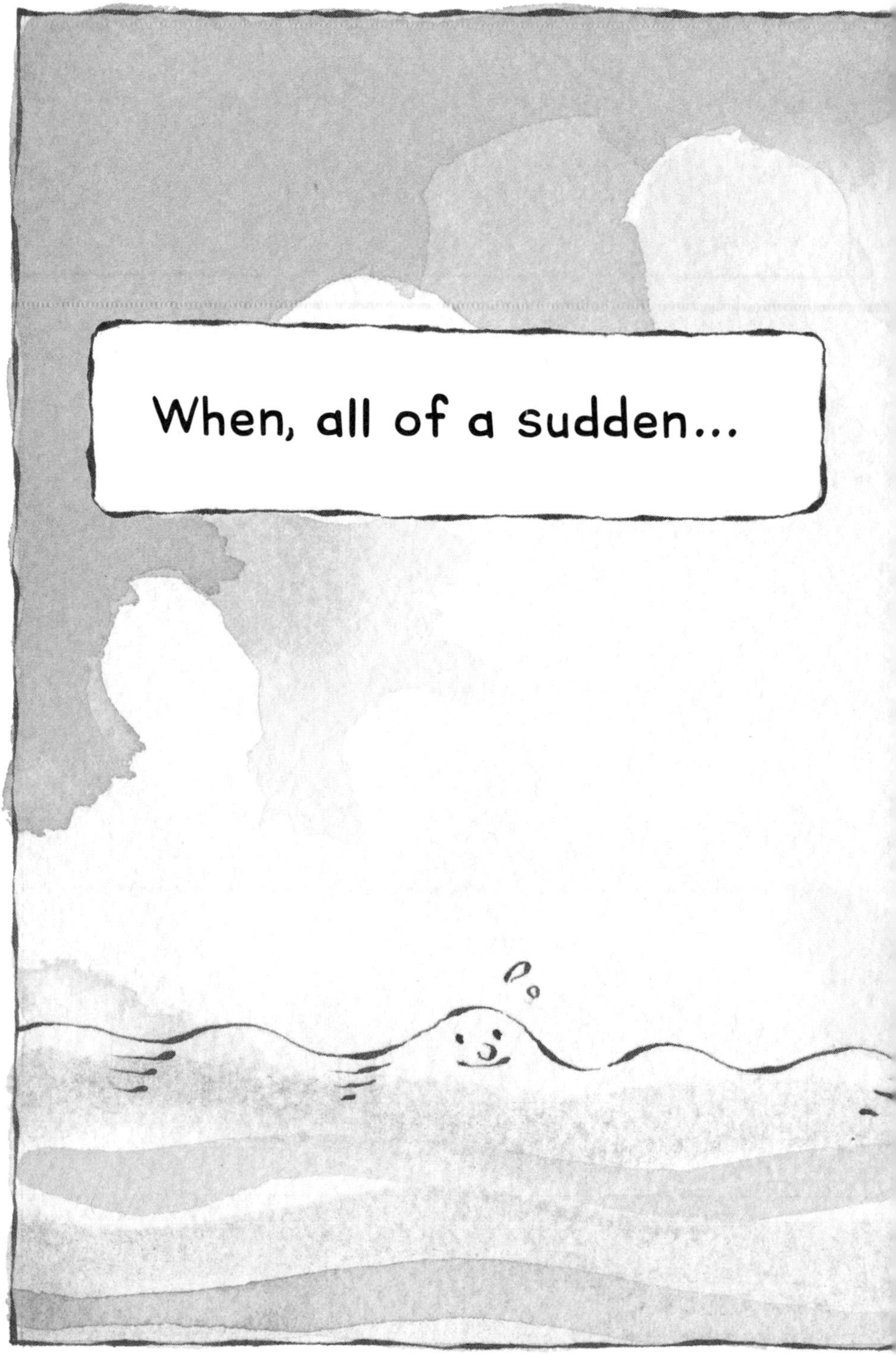
When, all of a sudden...

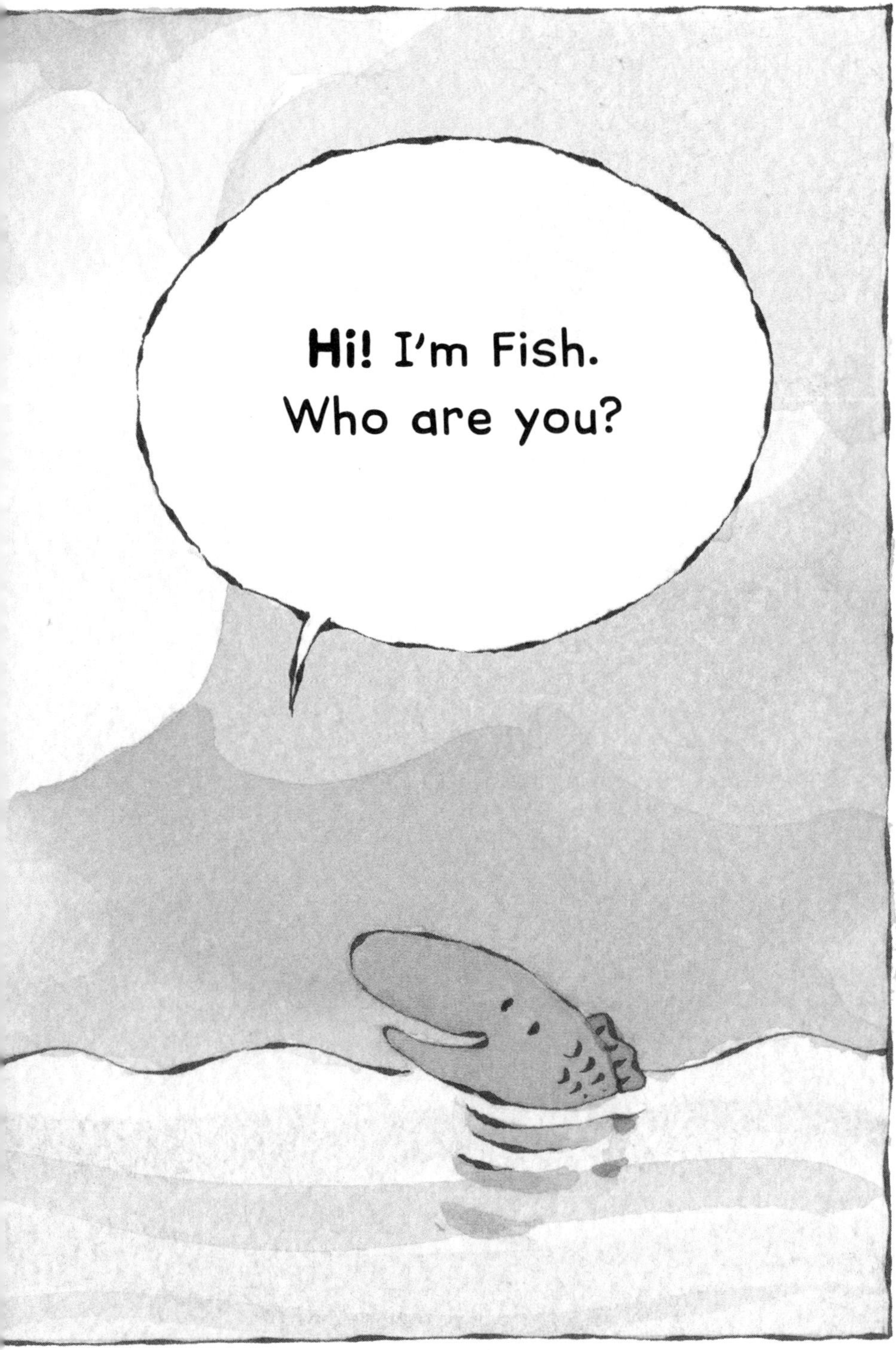
Hi! I'm Fish.
Who are you?

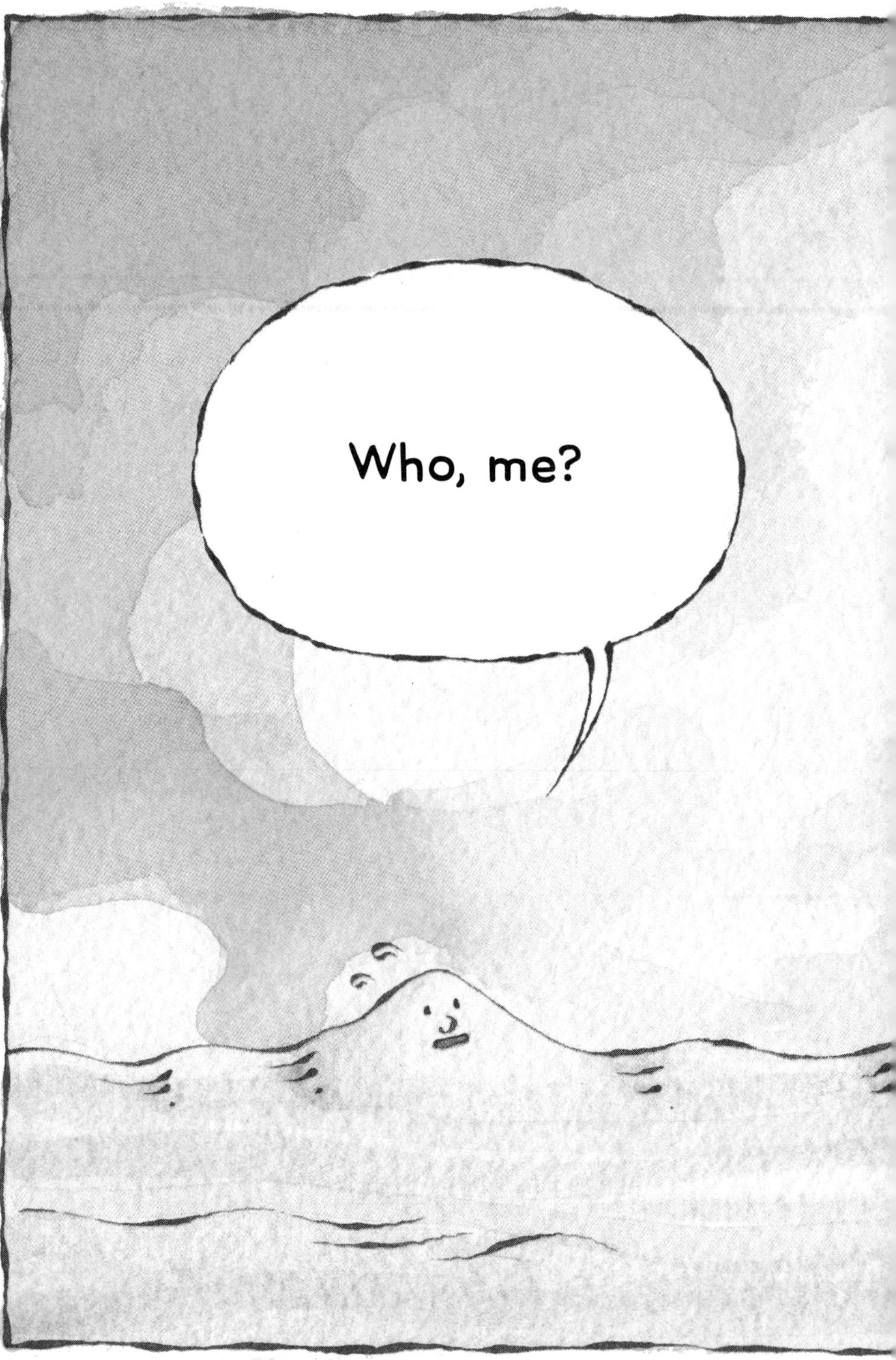
Who, me?

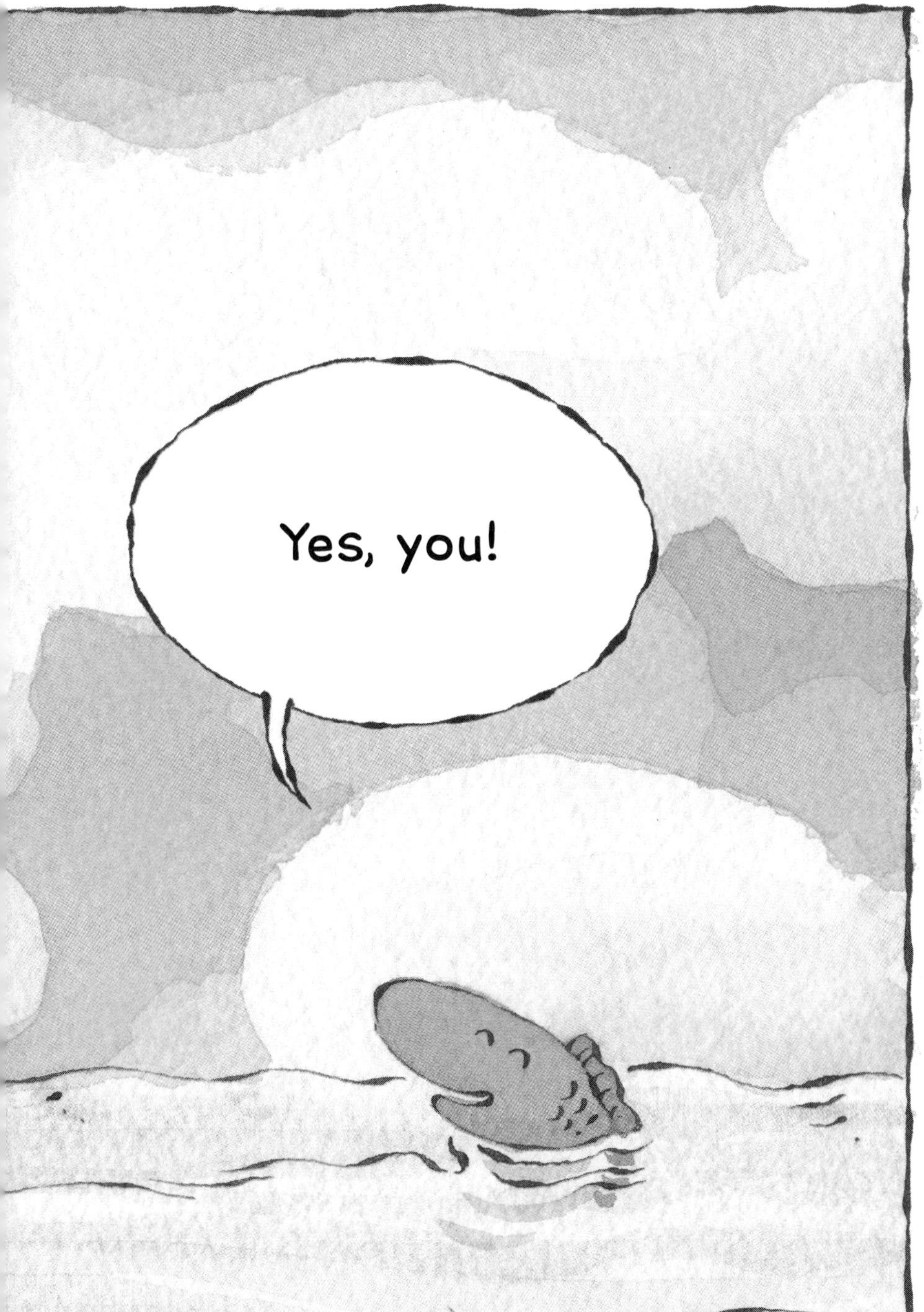
Yes, you!

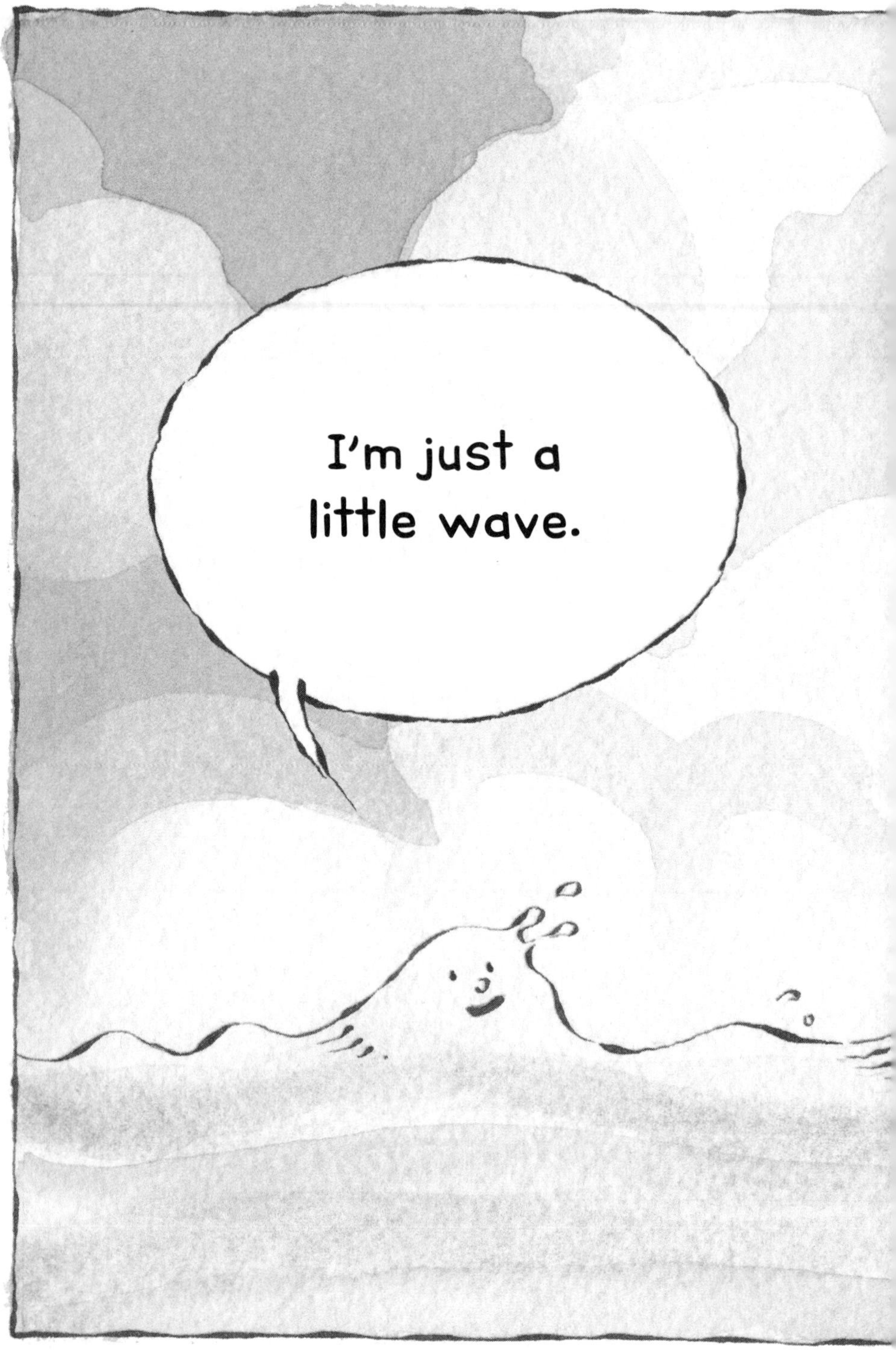
I'm just a little wave.

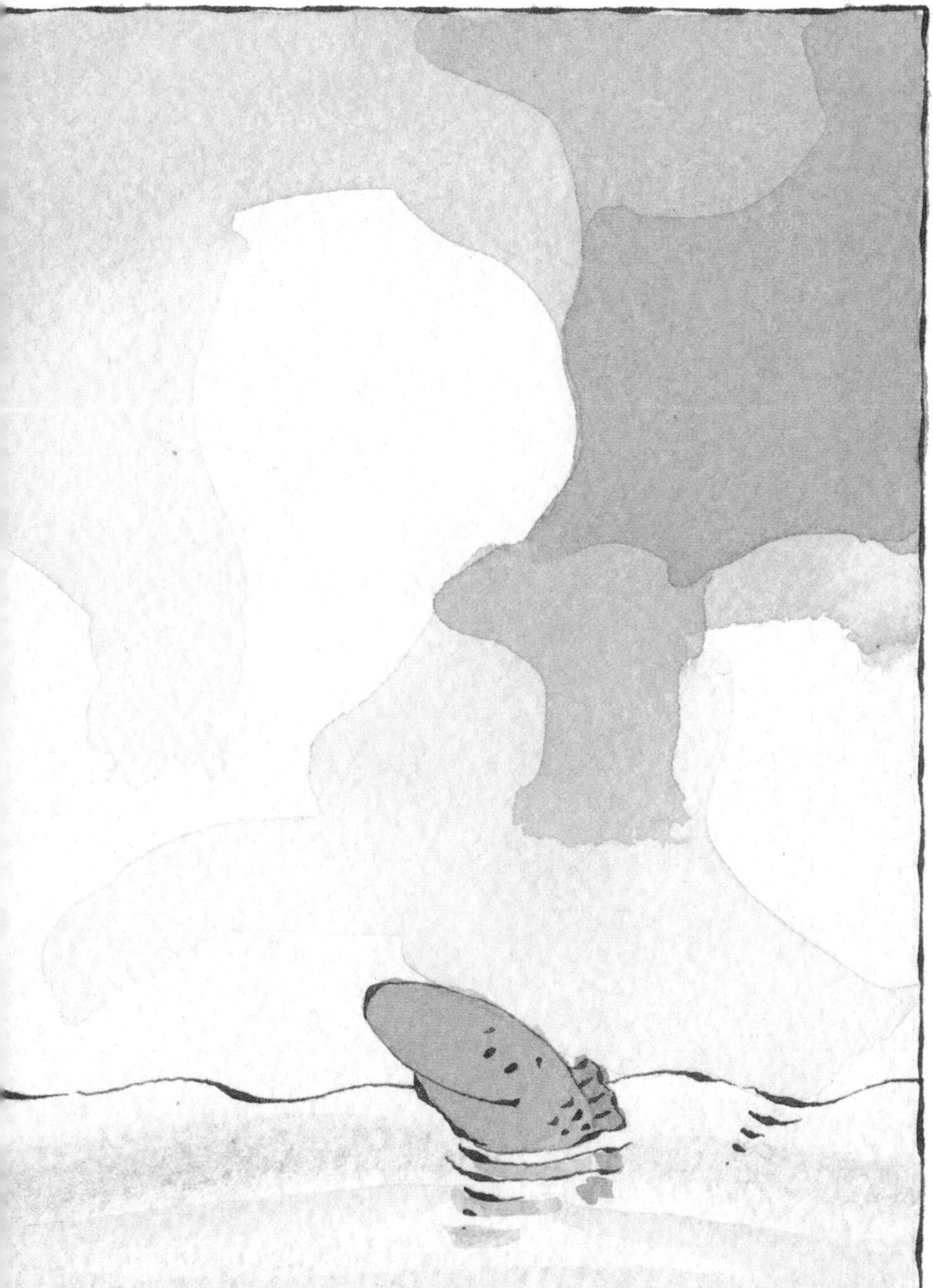

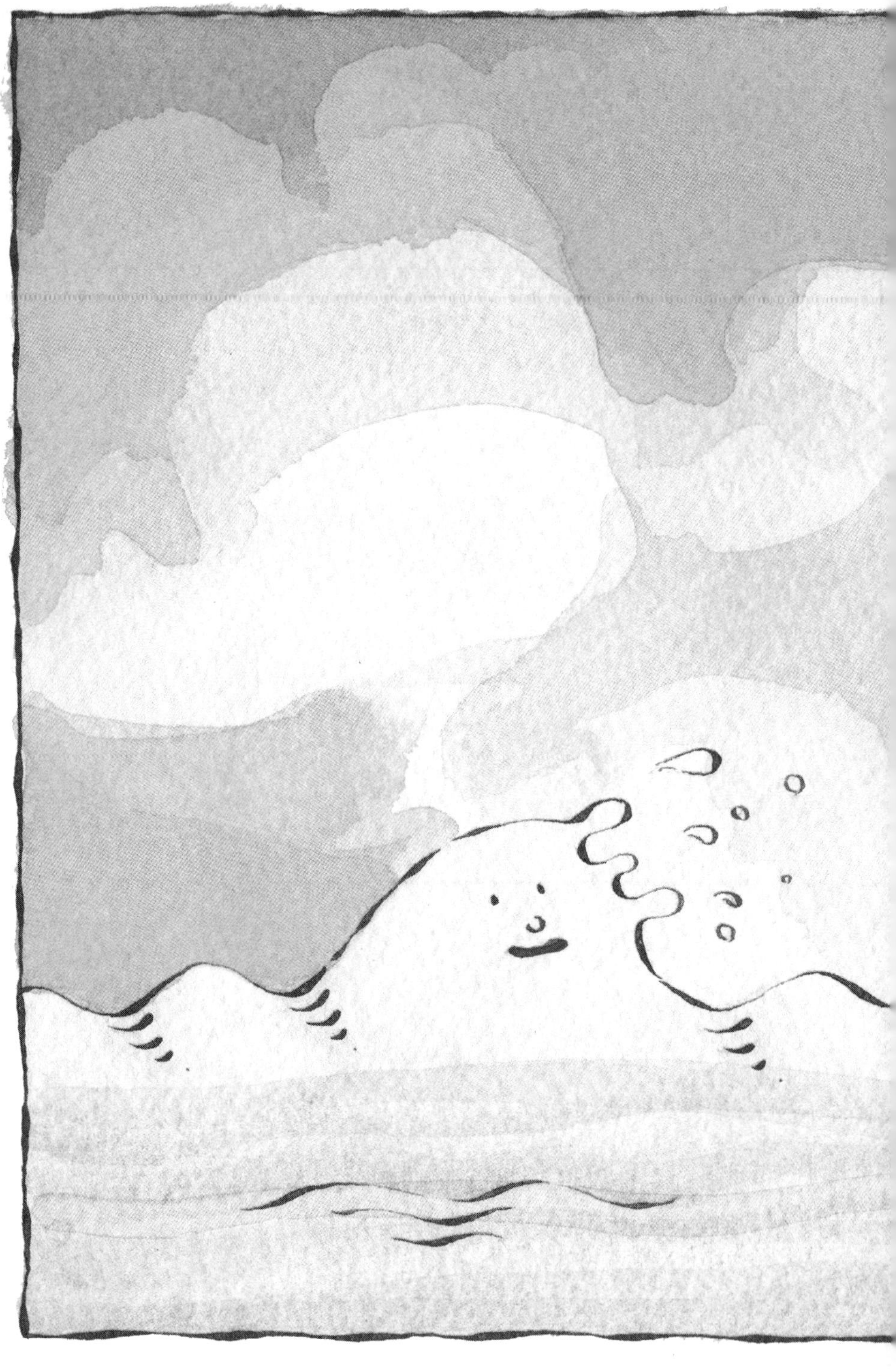

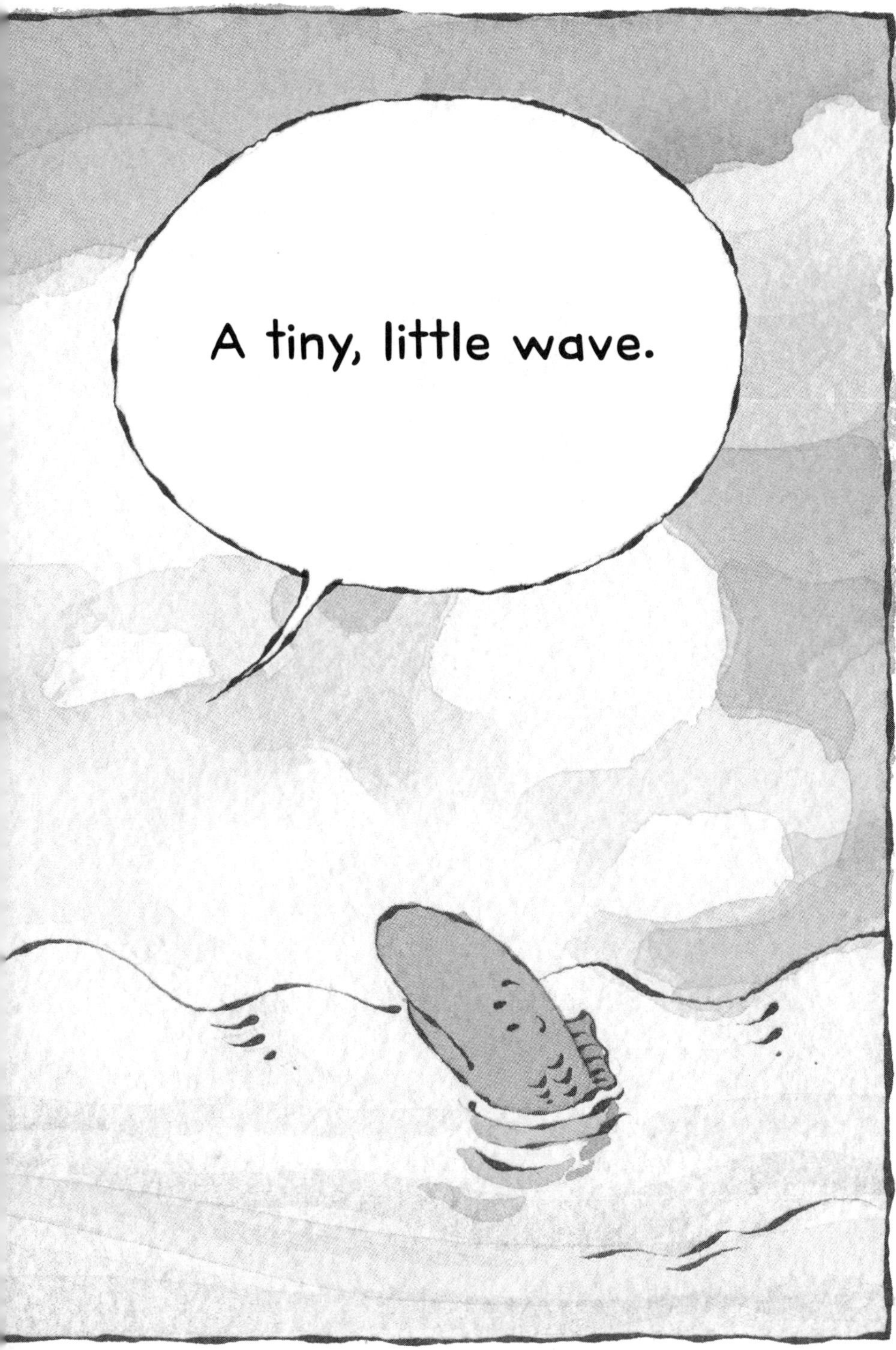
A tiny, little wave.

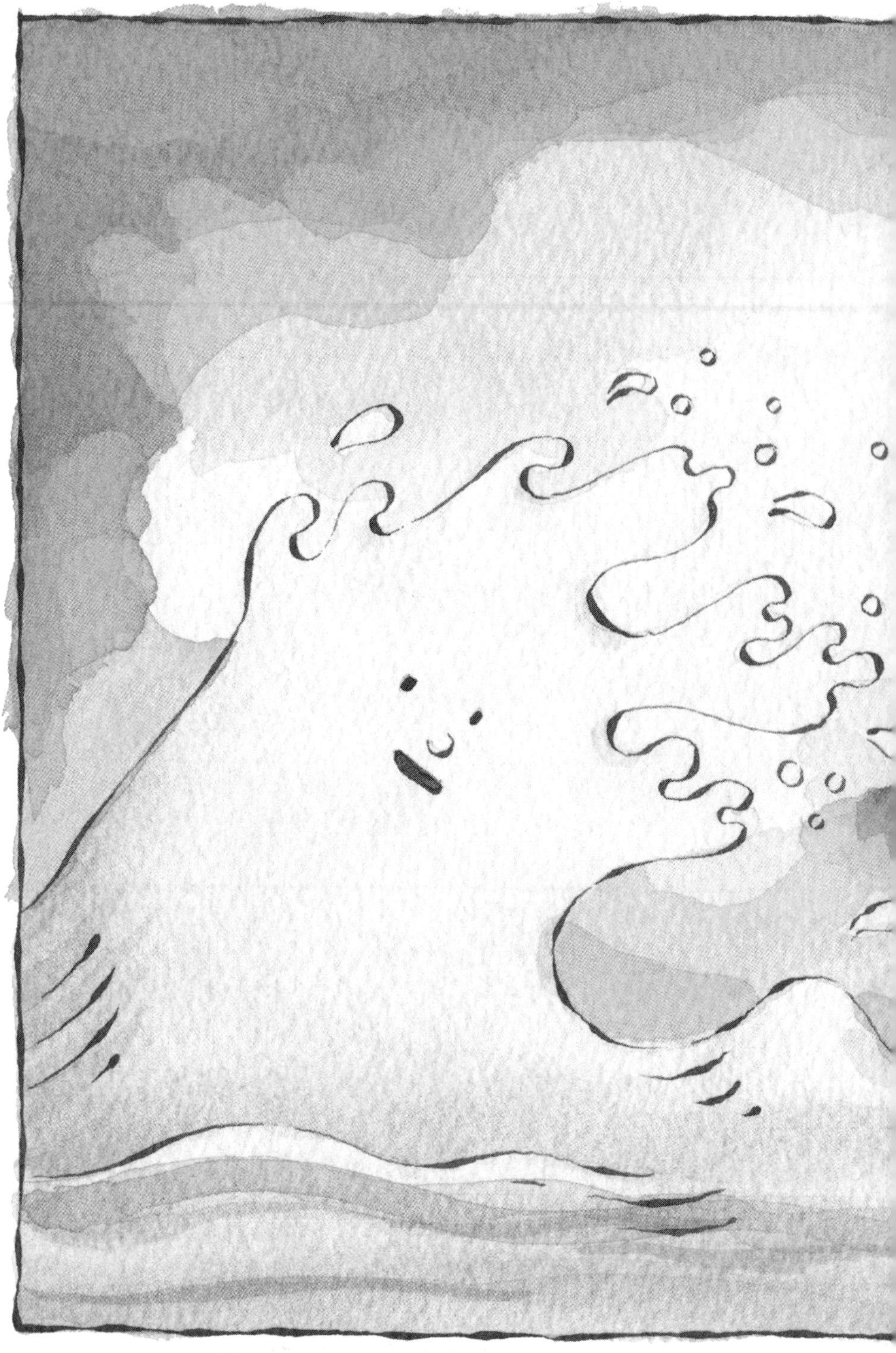

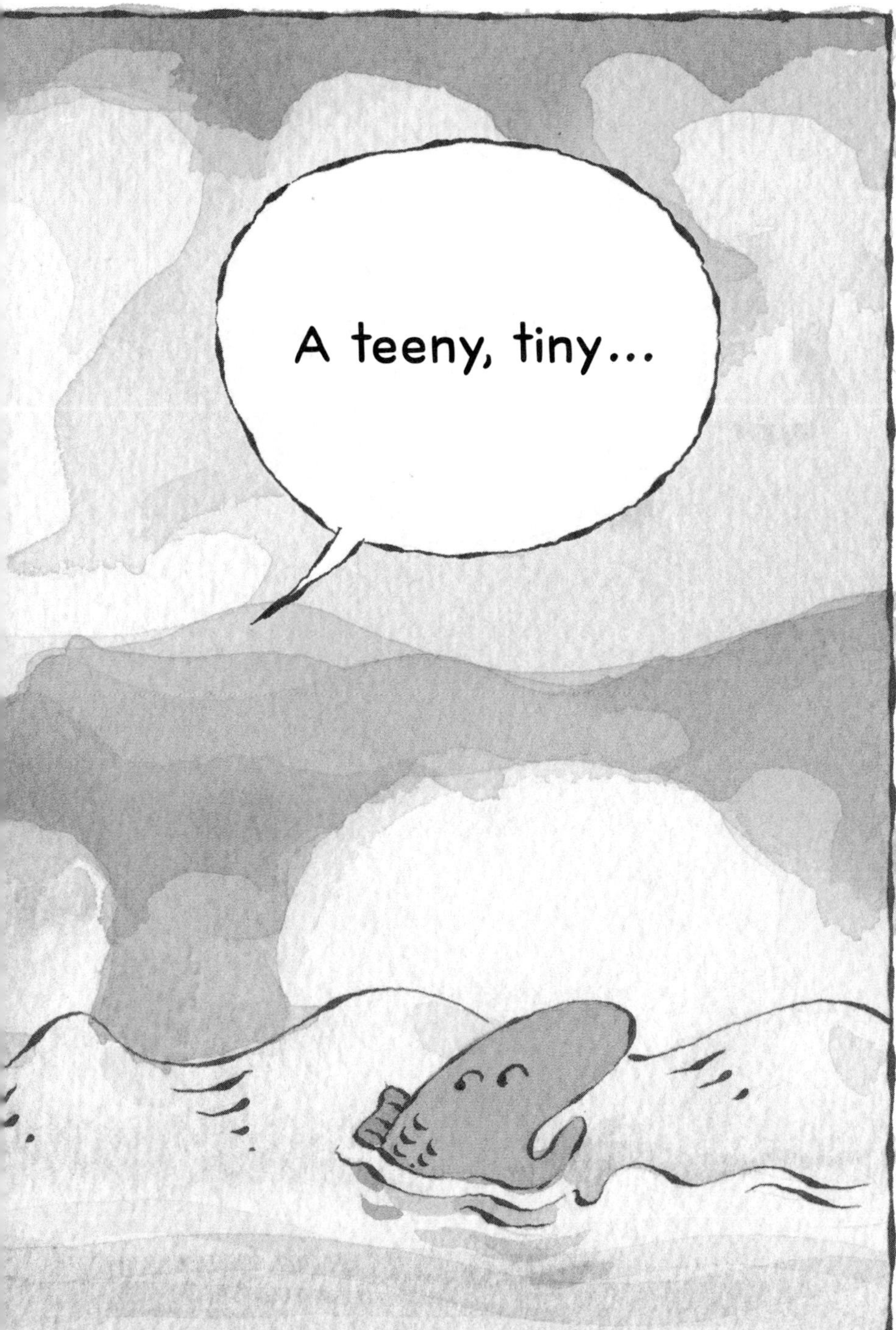
A teeny, tiny...

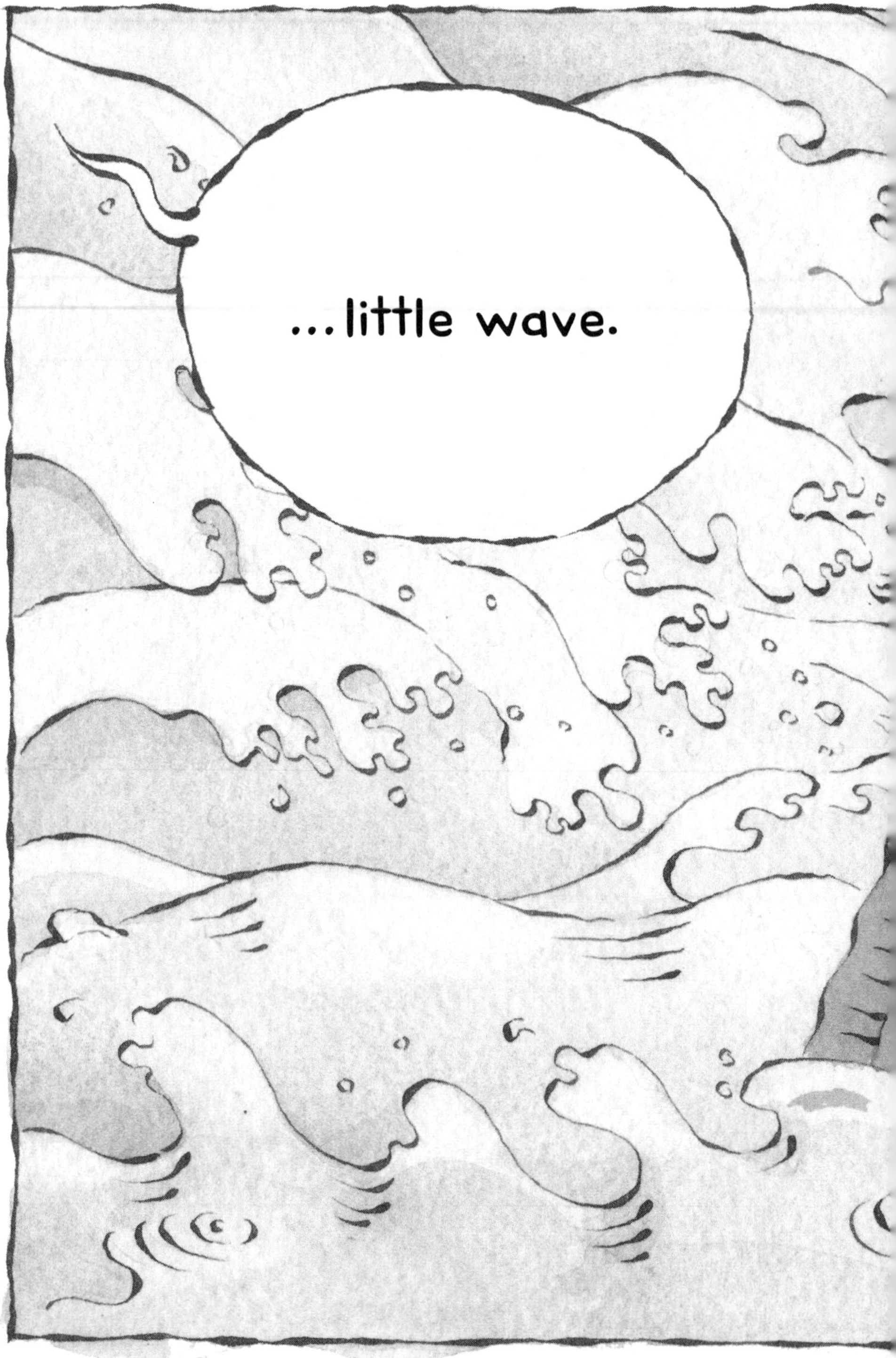
...little wave.

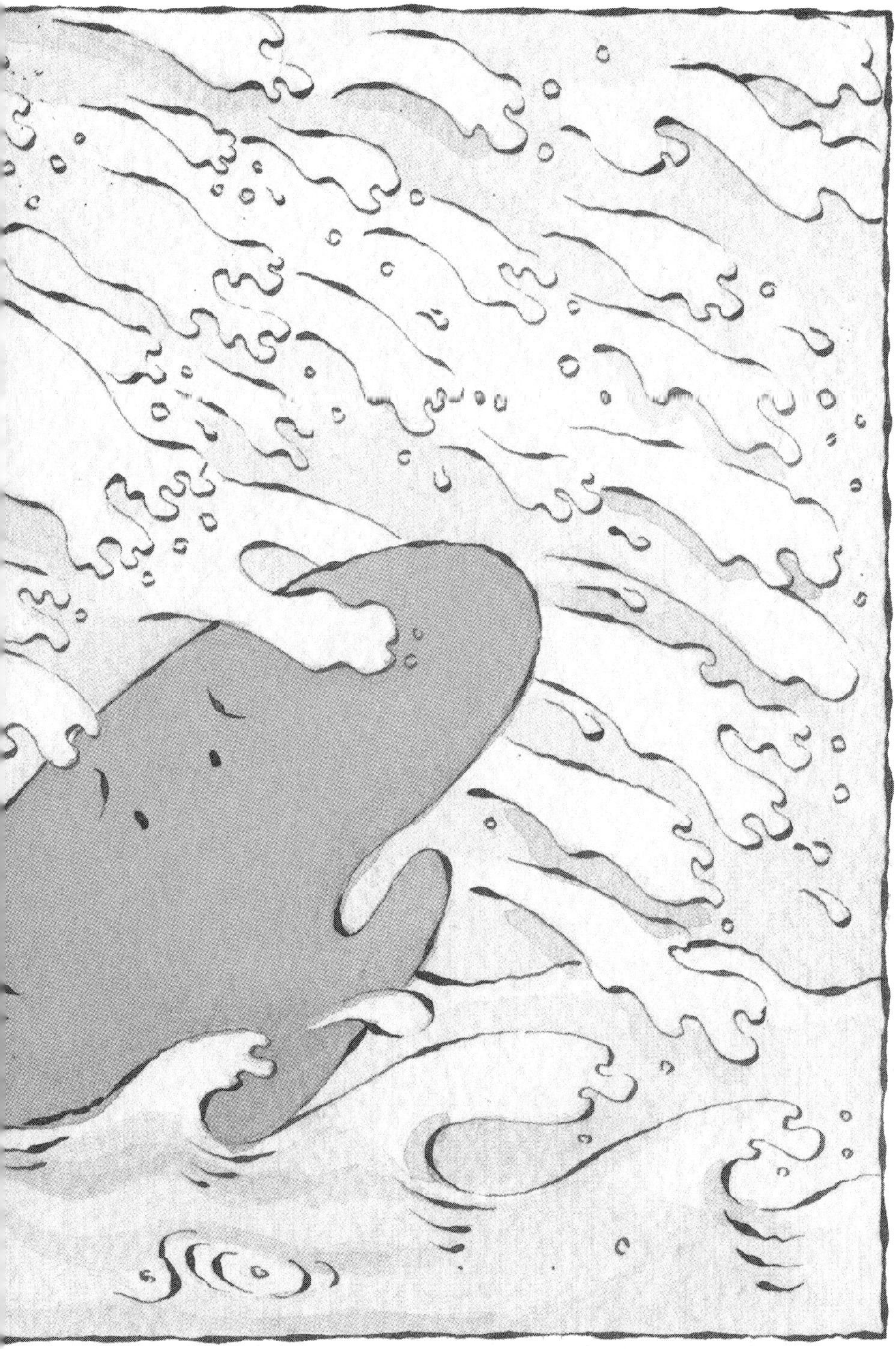

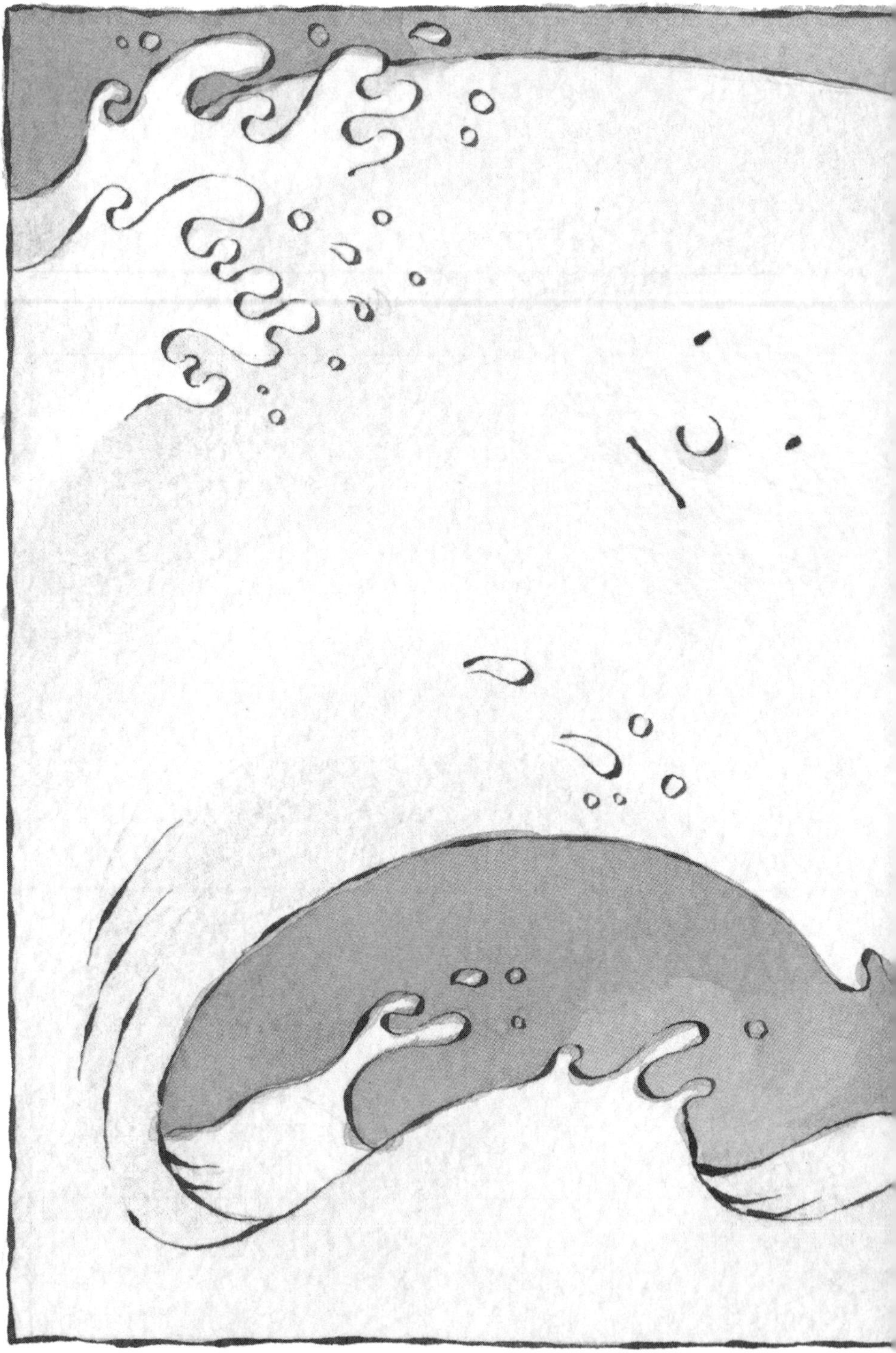

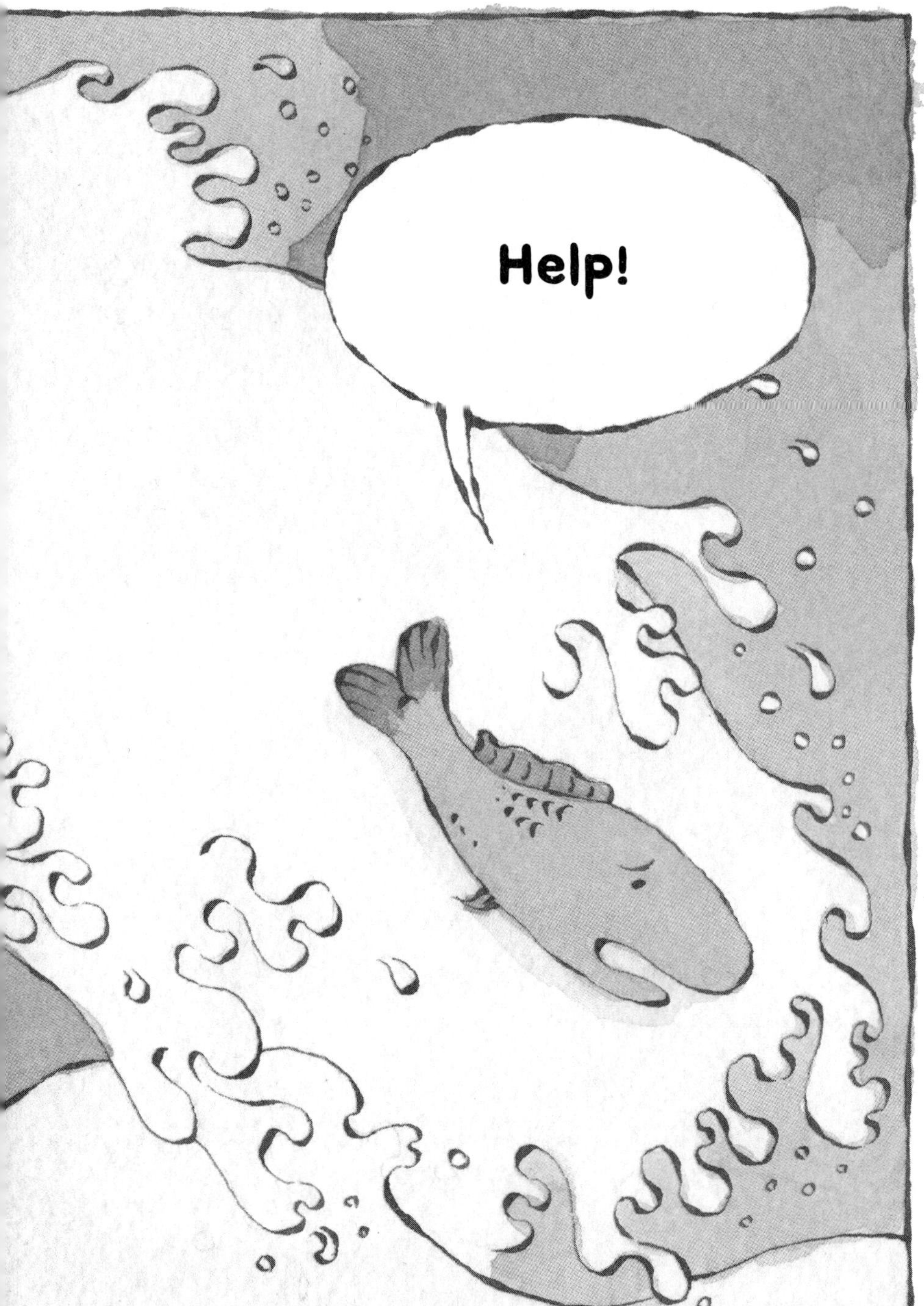
Help!

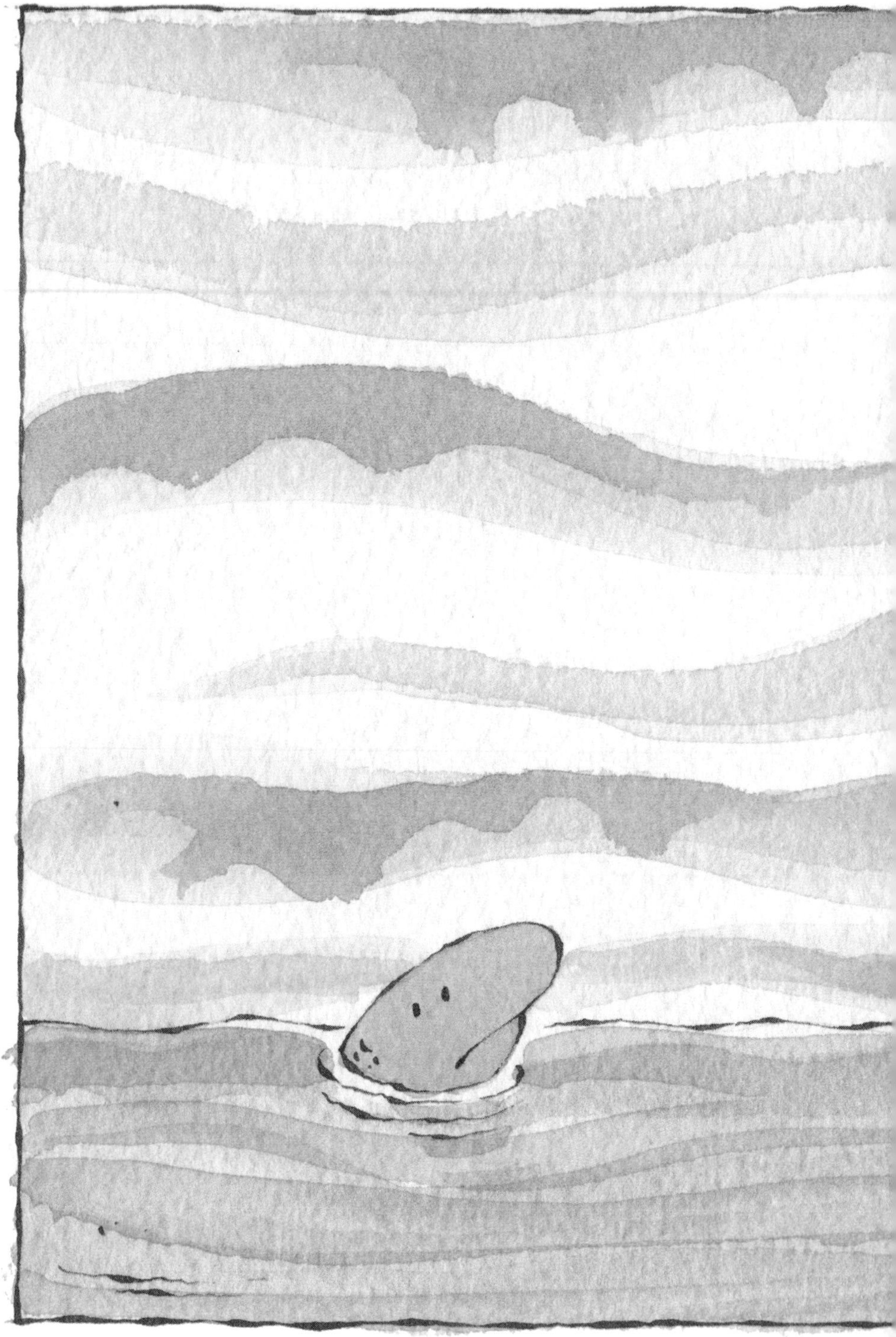

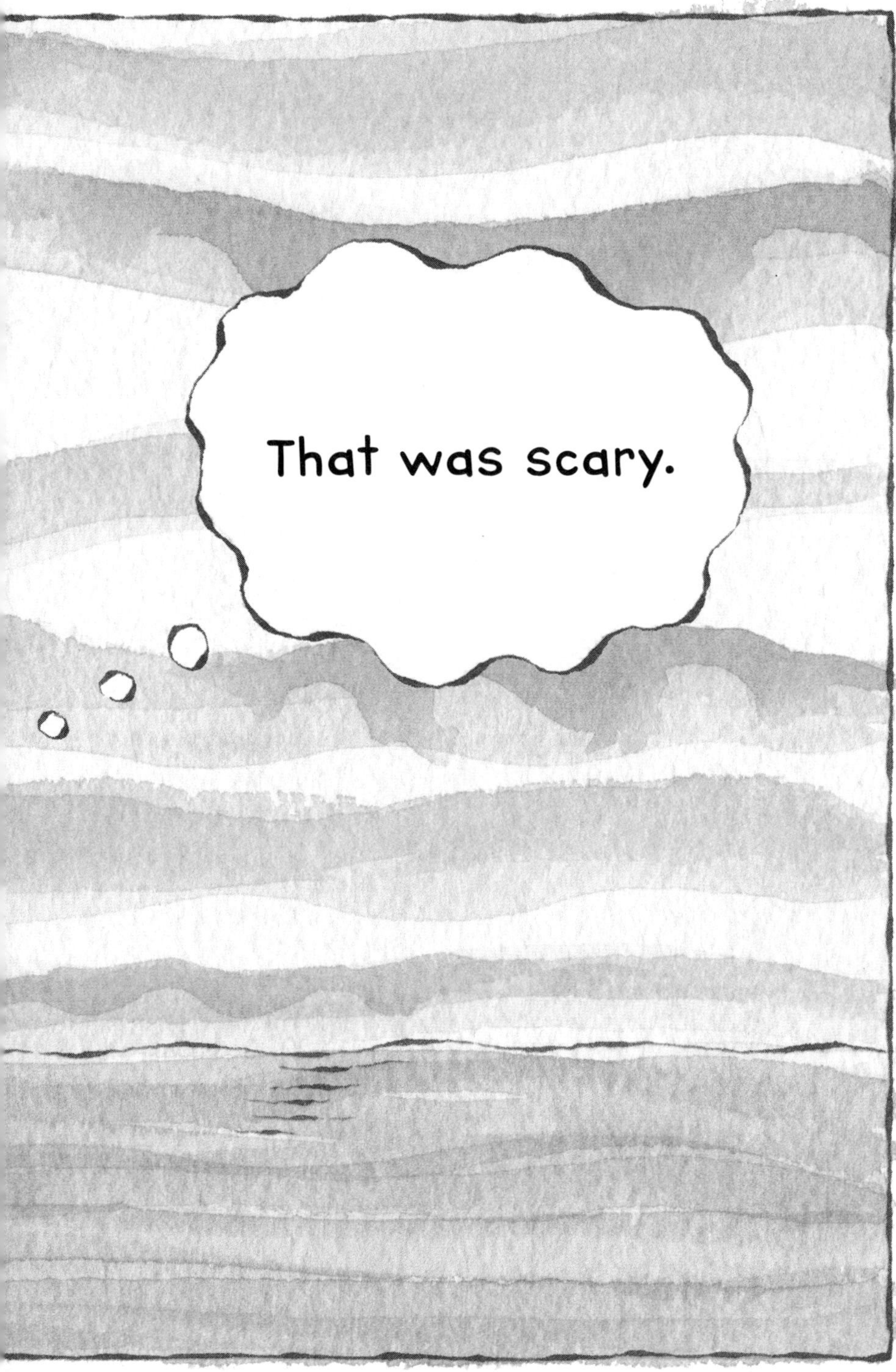
That was scary.

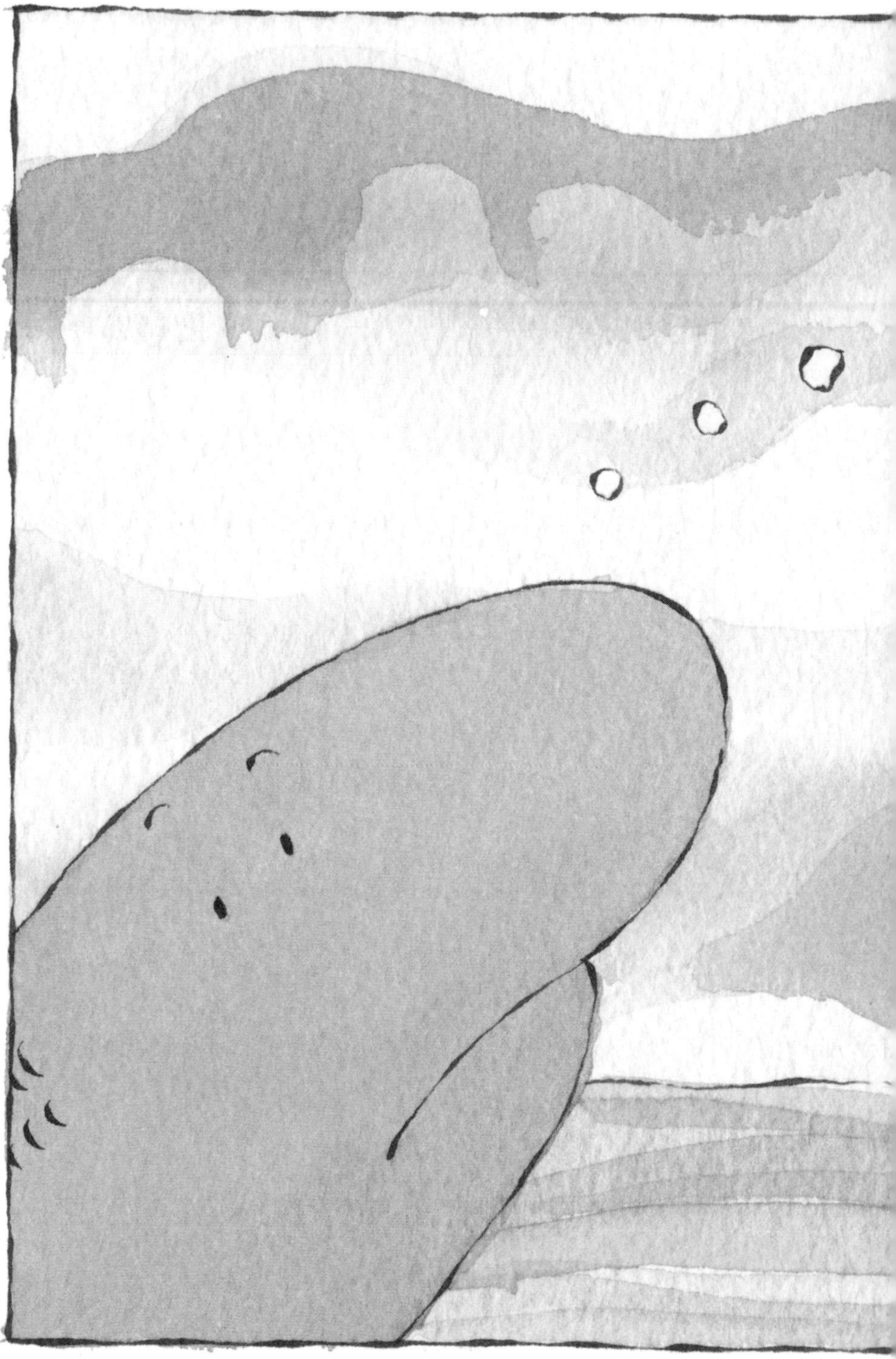

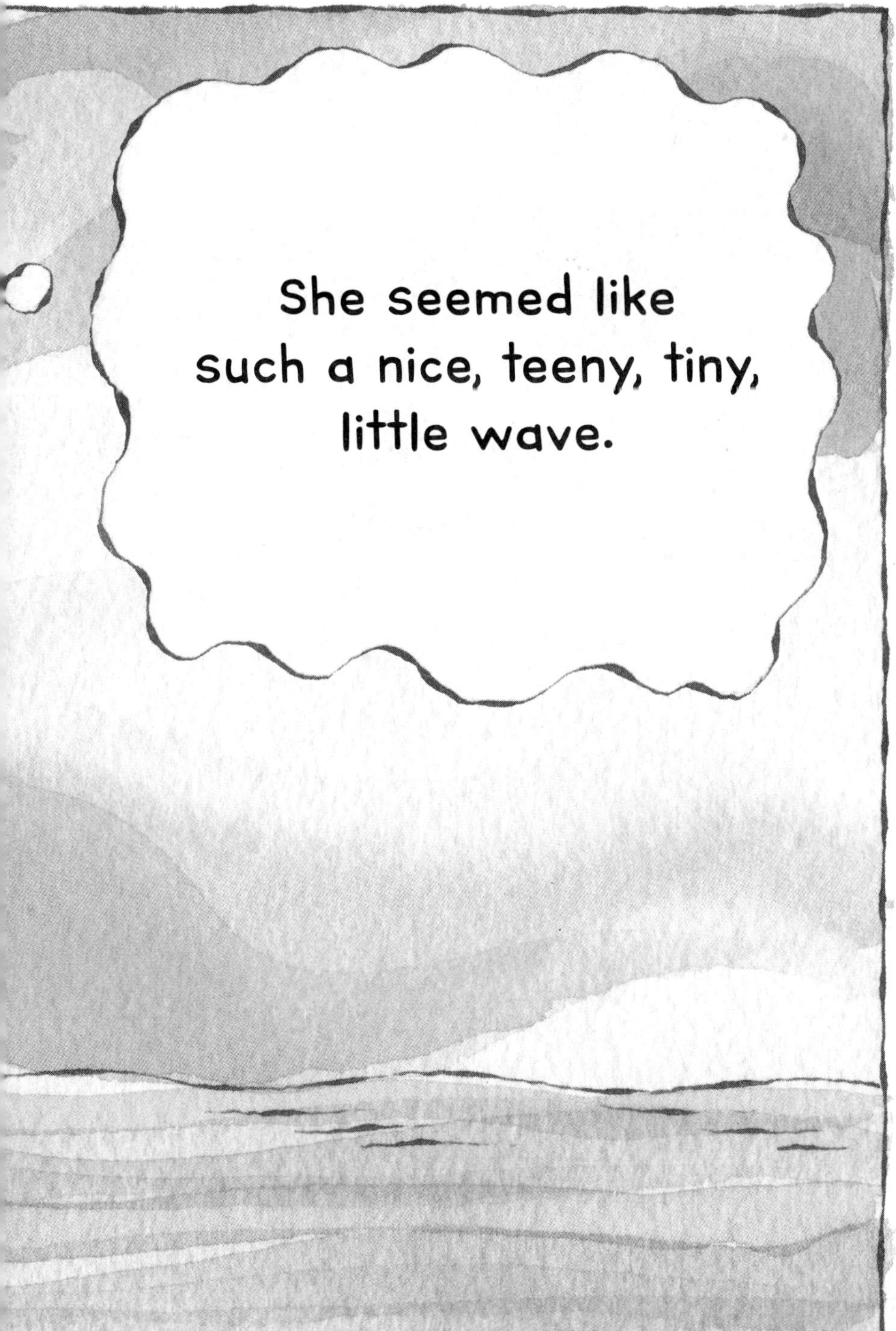
She seemed like
such a nice, teeny, tiny,
little wave.

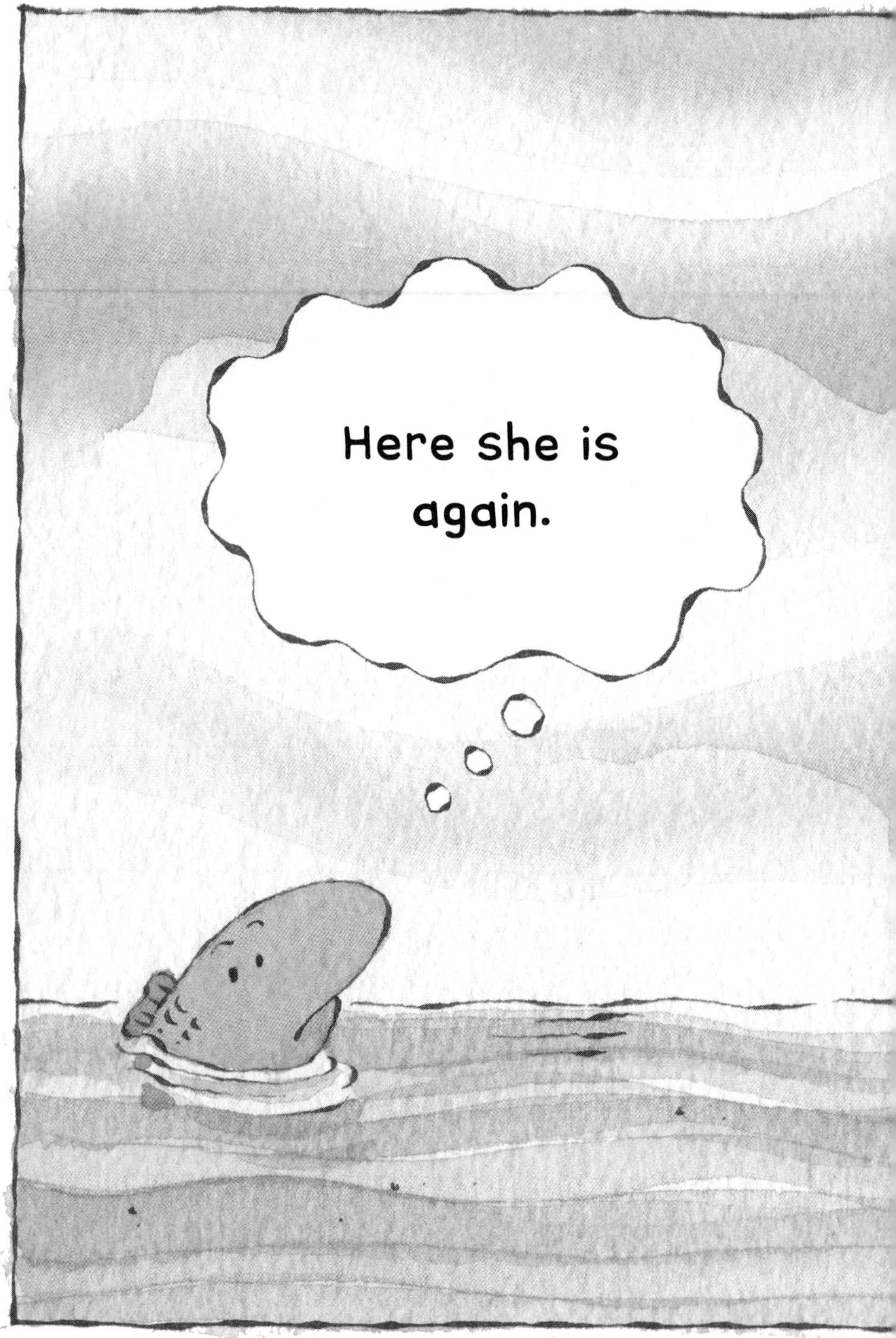
Here she is
again.

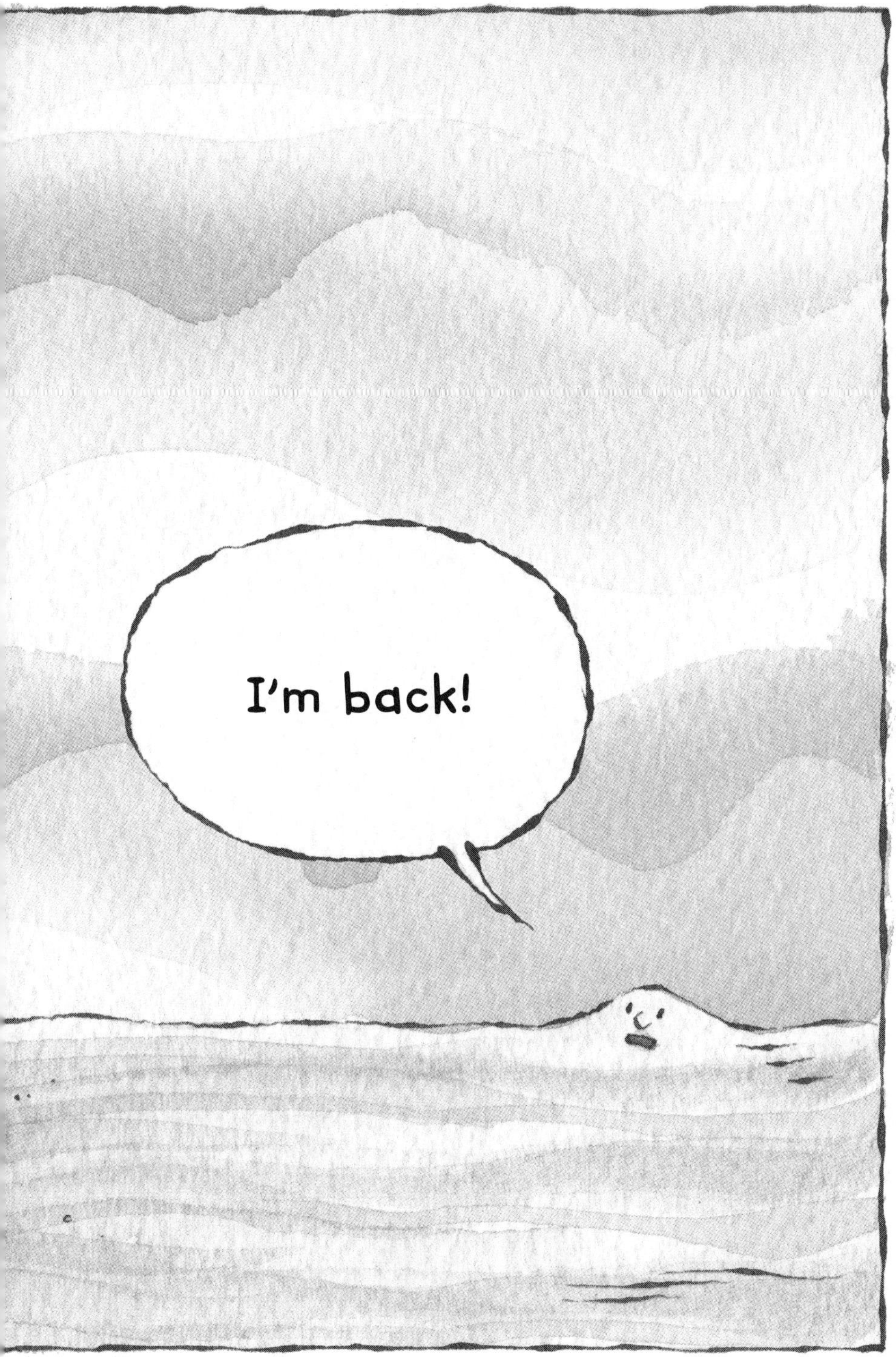
I'm back!

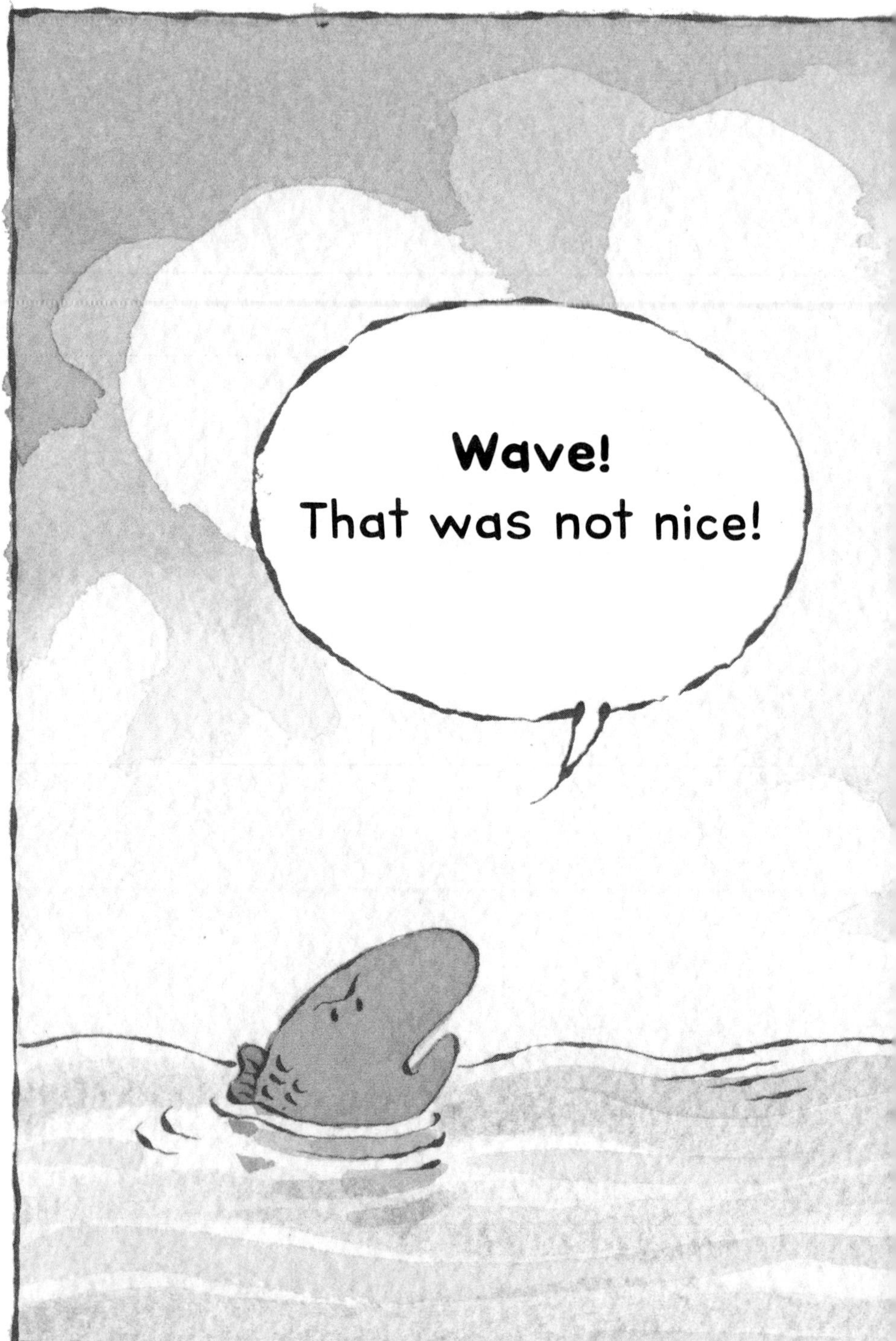
Wave!
That was not nice!

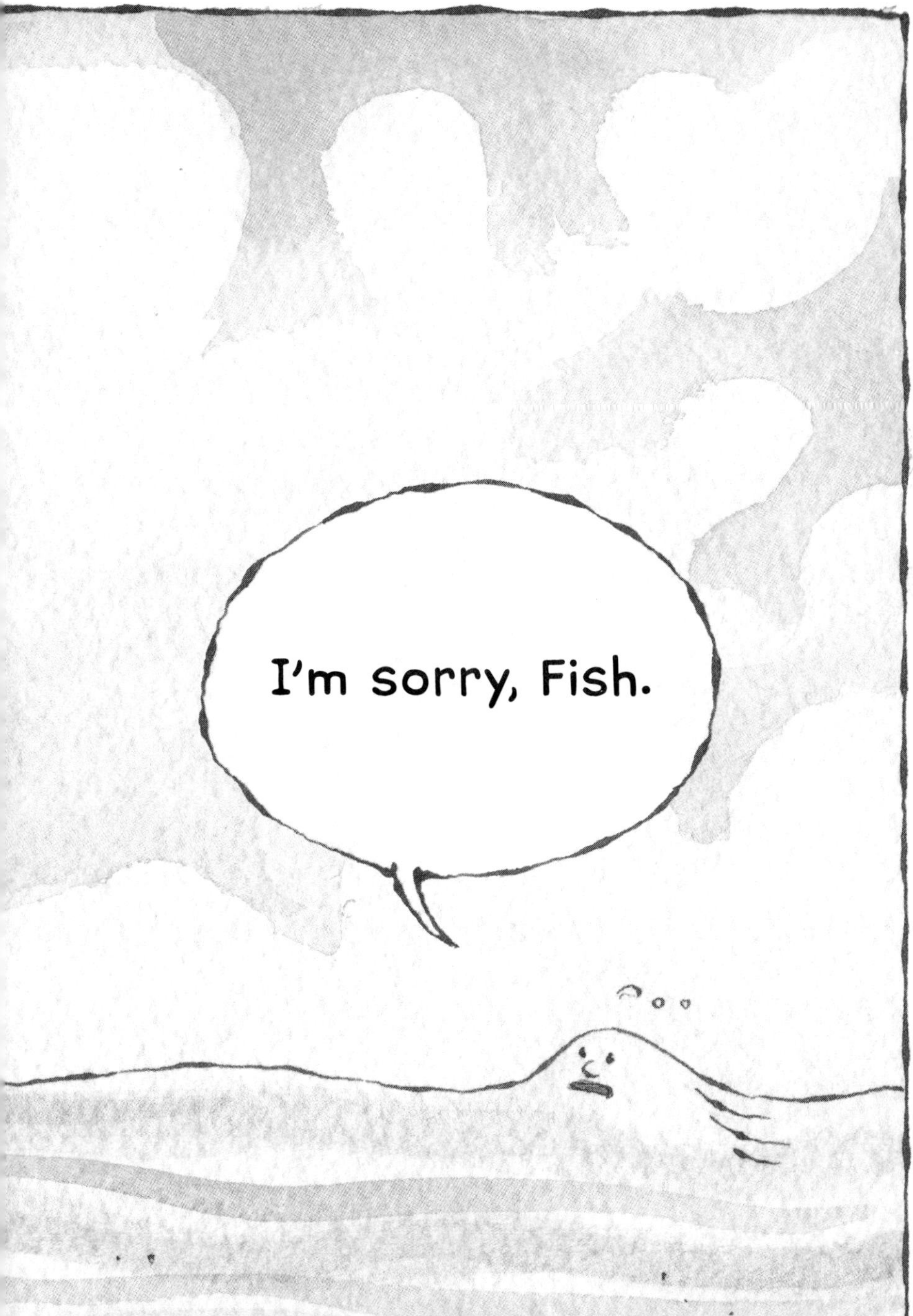
I'm sorry, Fish.

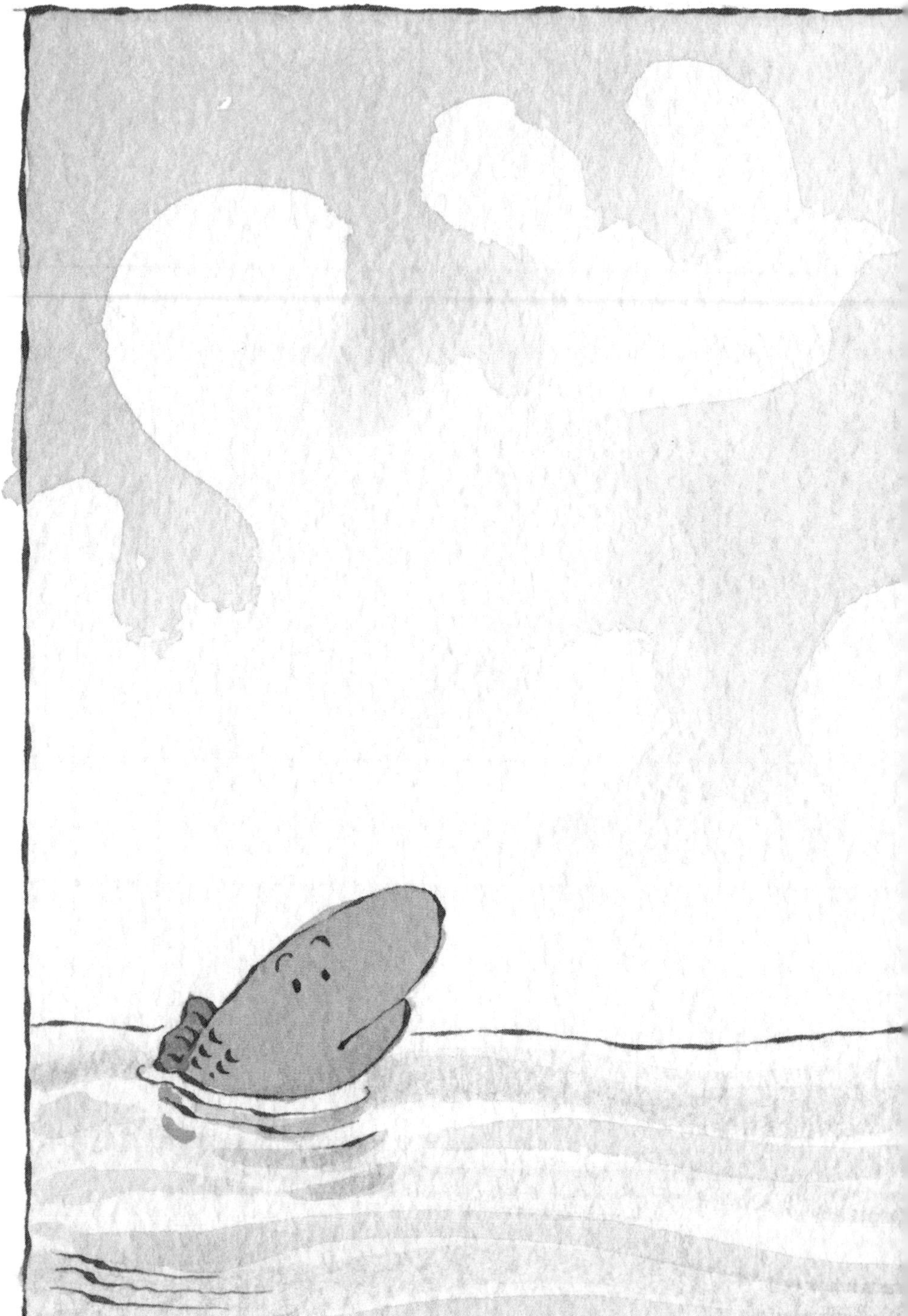

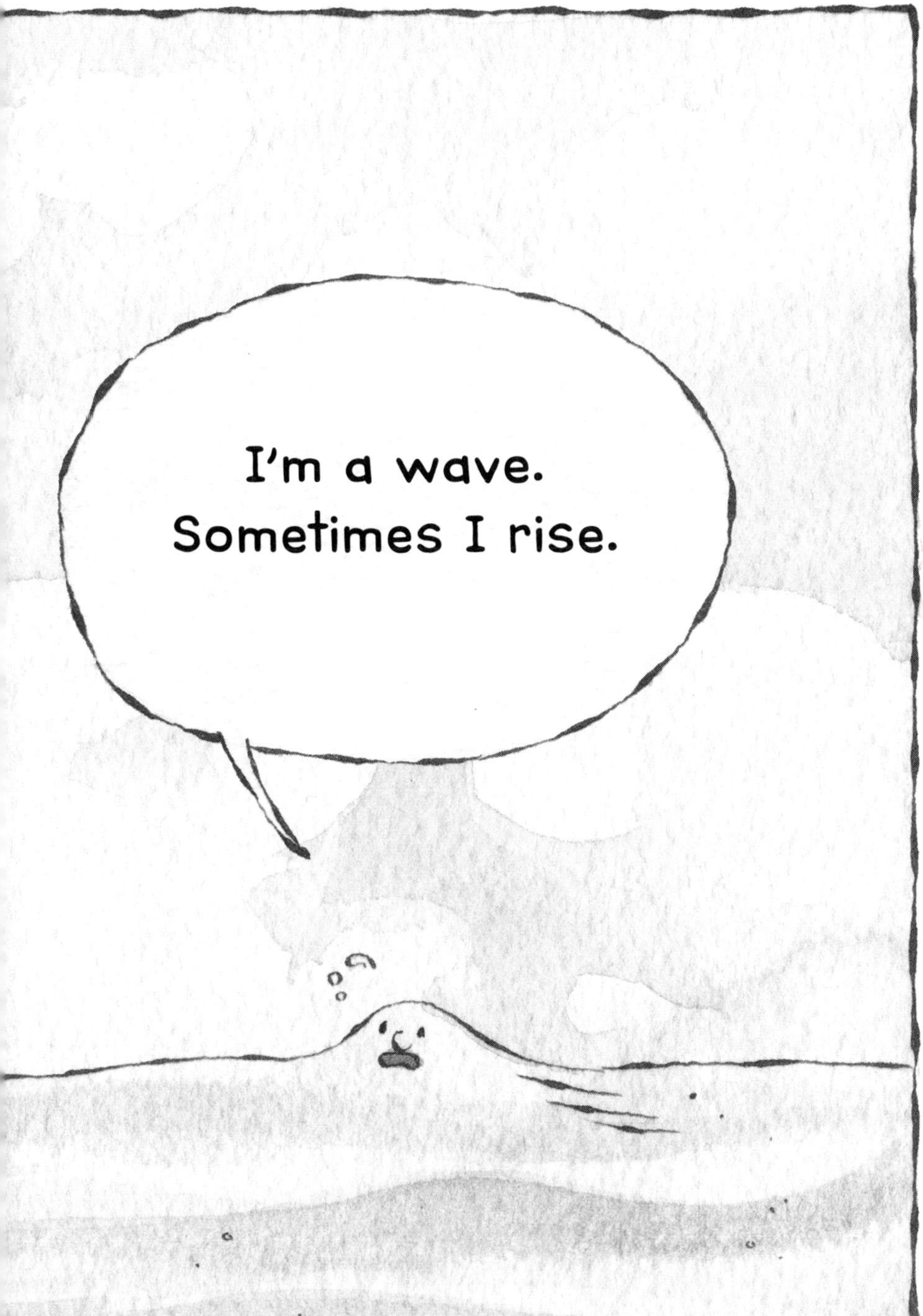
I'm a wave.
Sometimes I rise.

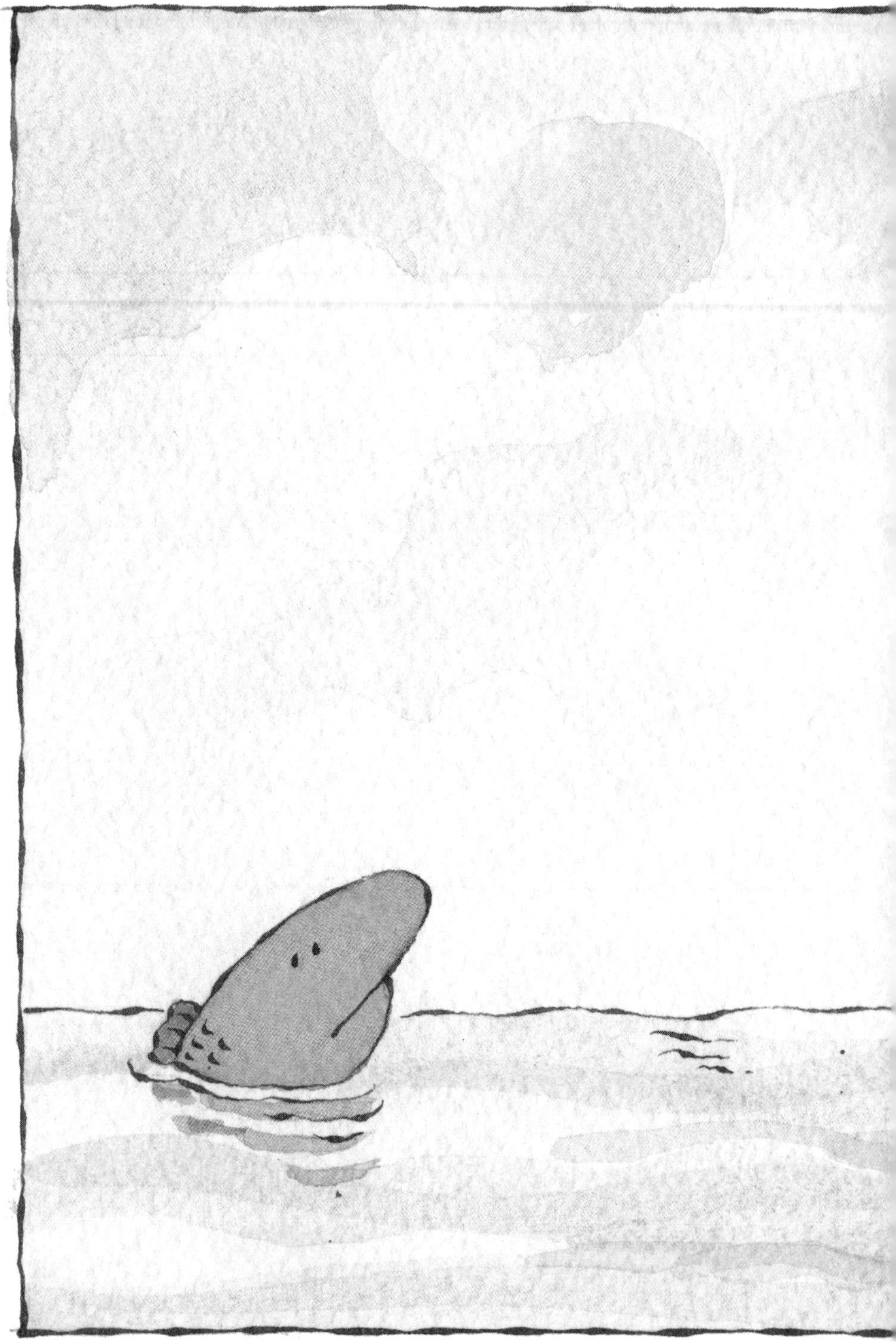

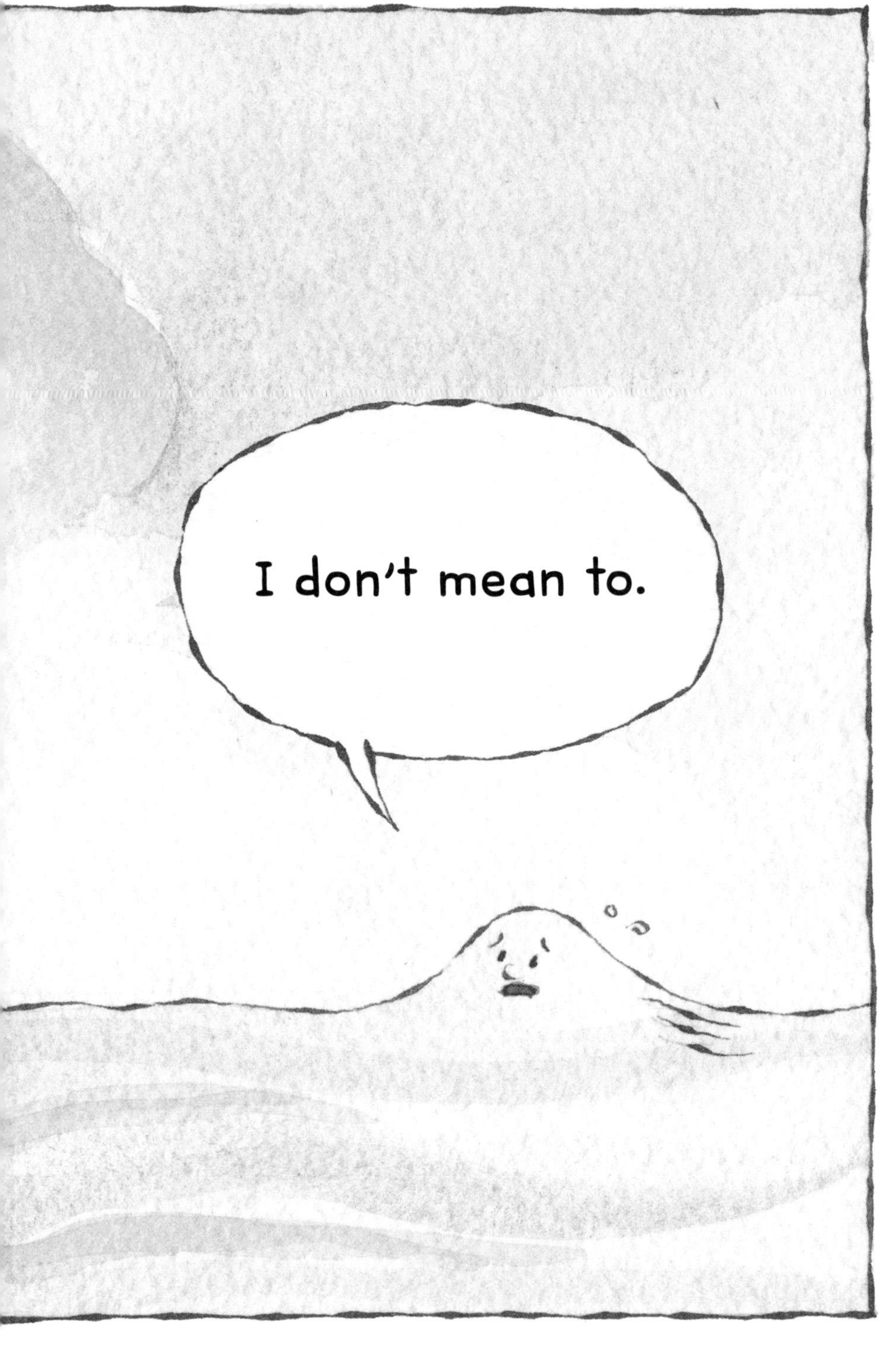
I don't mean to.

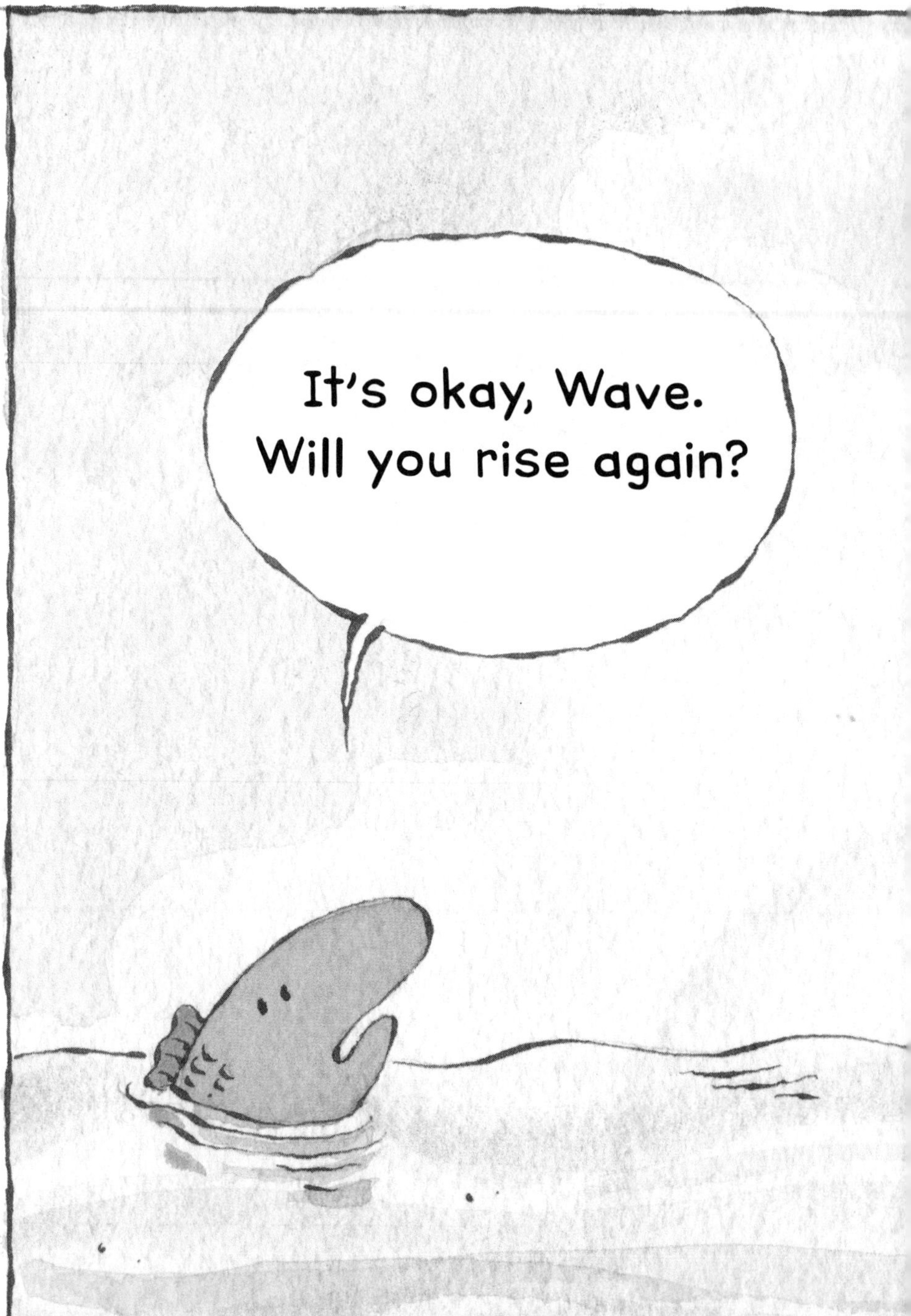
It's okay, Wave.
Will you rise again?

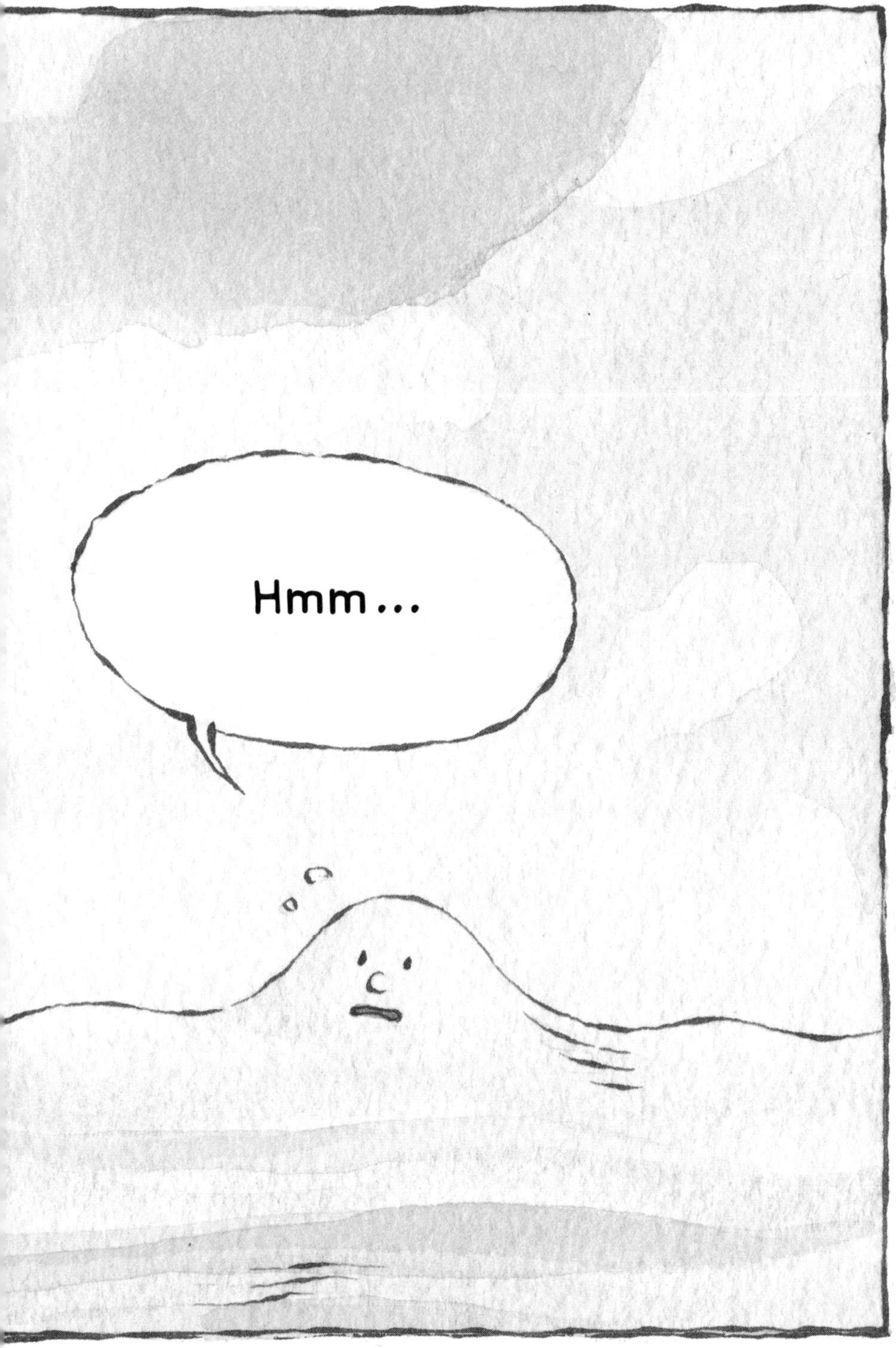
Hmm...

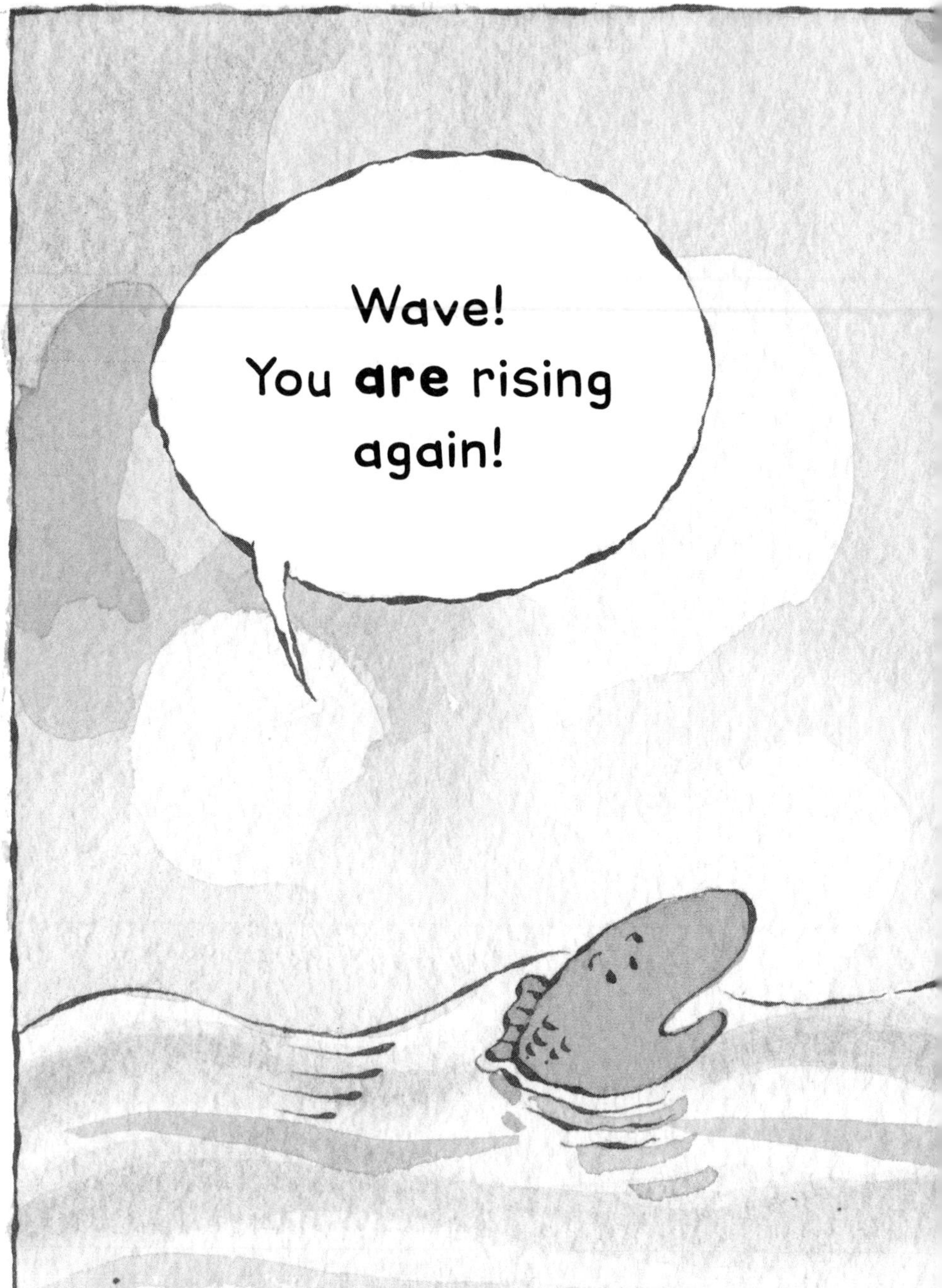
Wave! You **are** rising again!

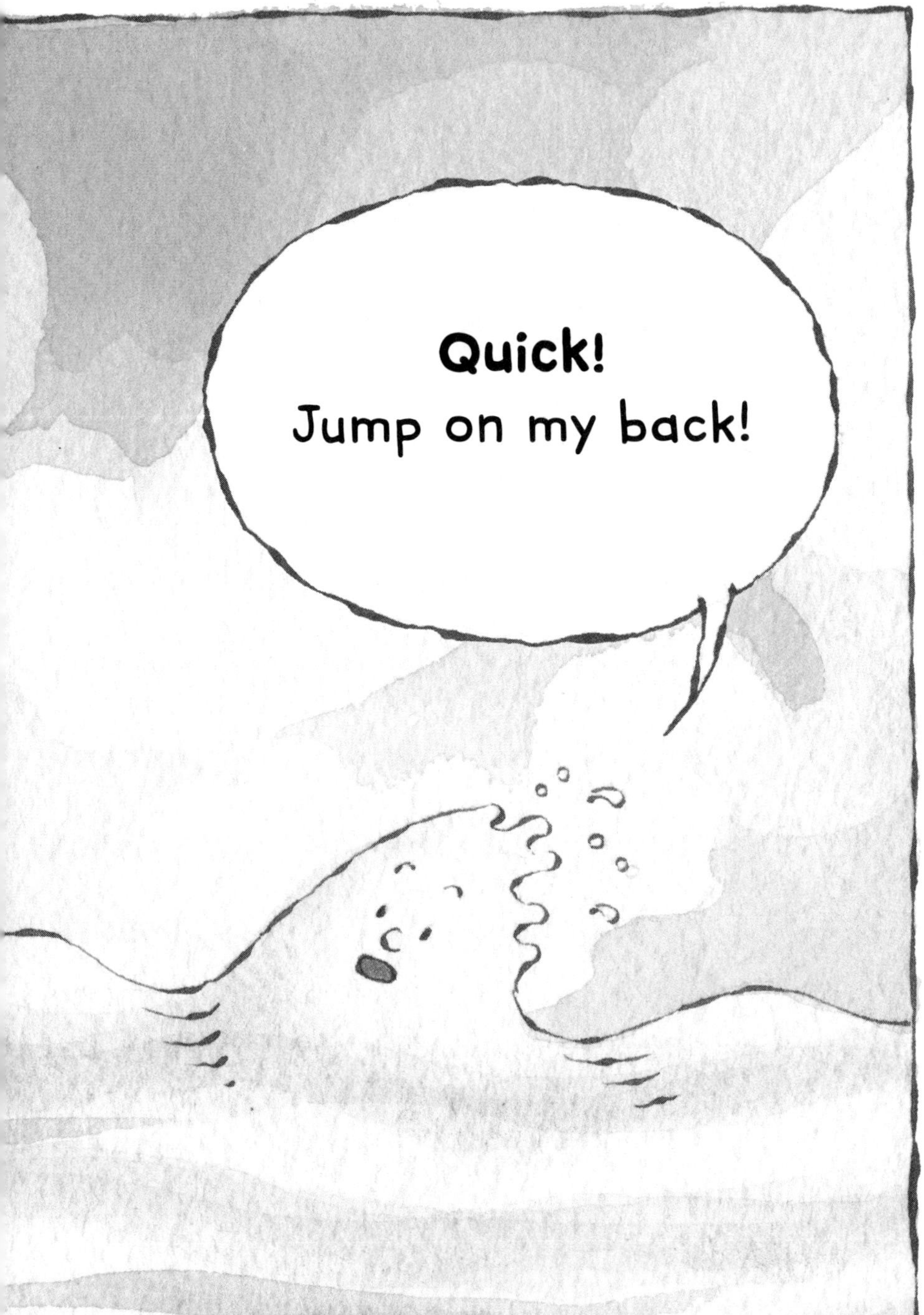
Quick!
Jump on my back!

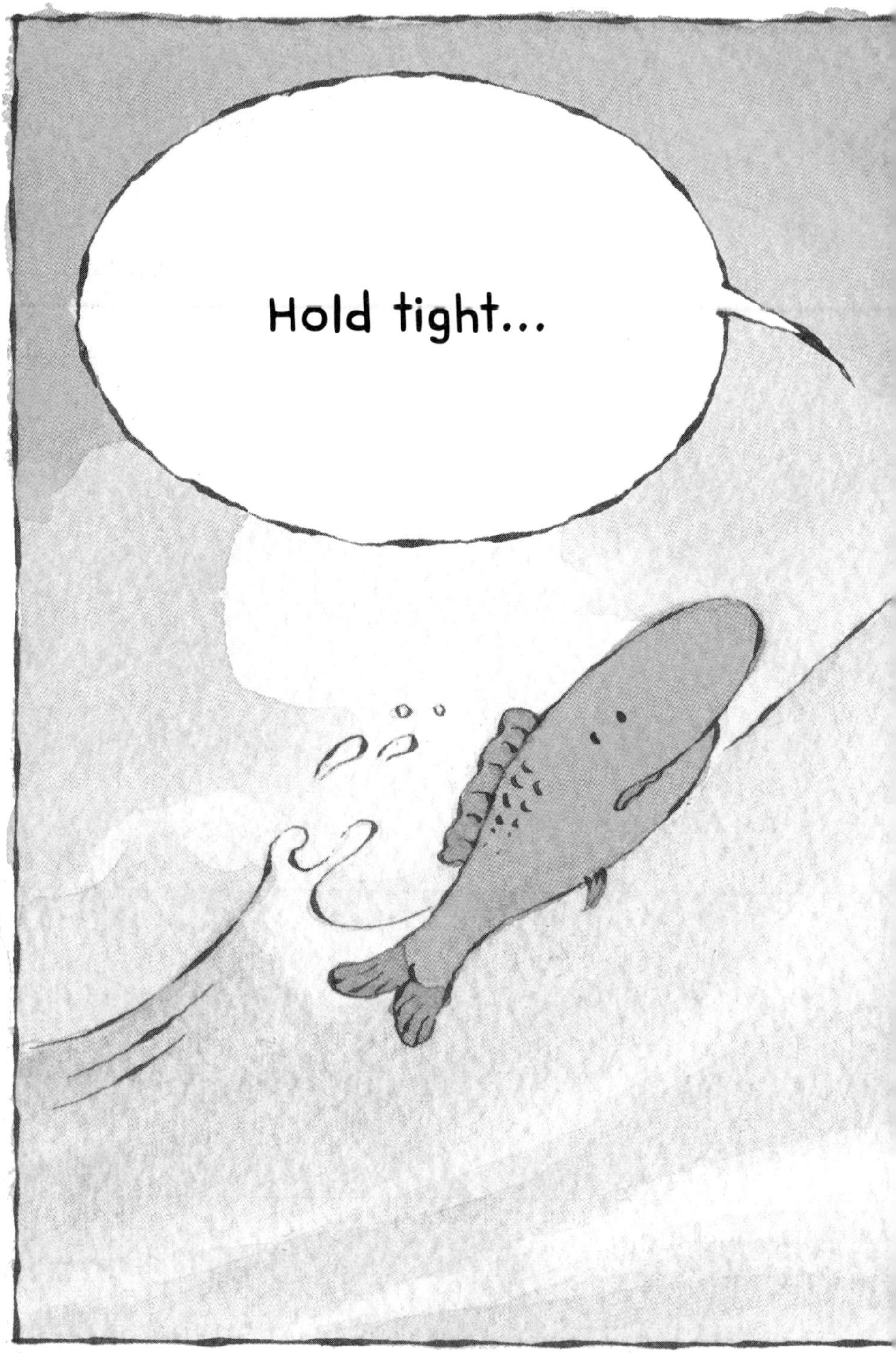
Hold tight...

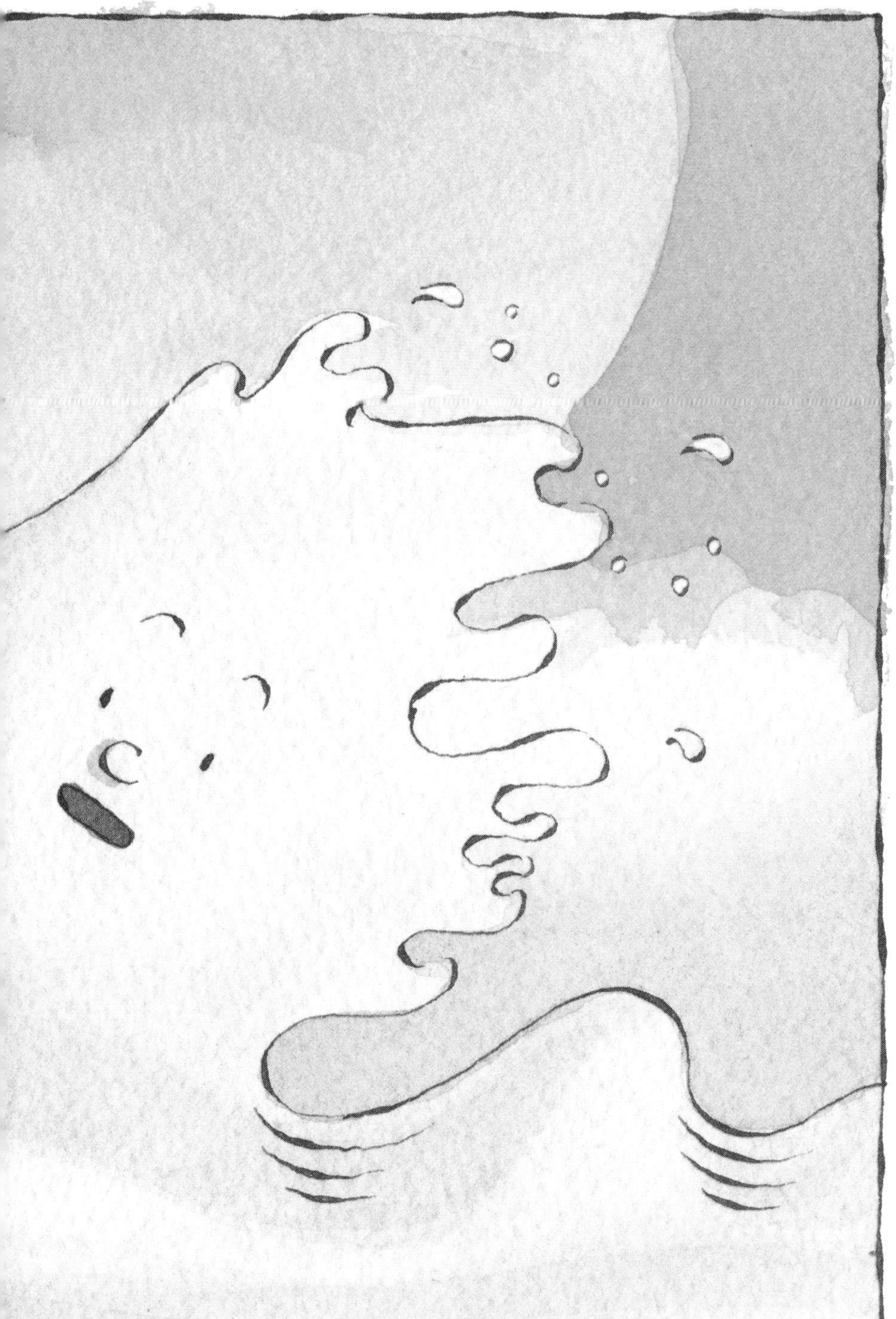

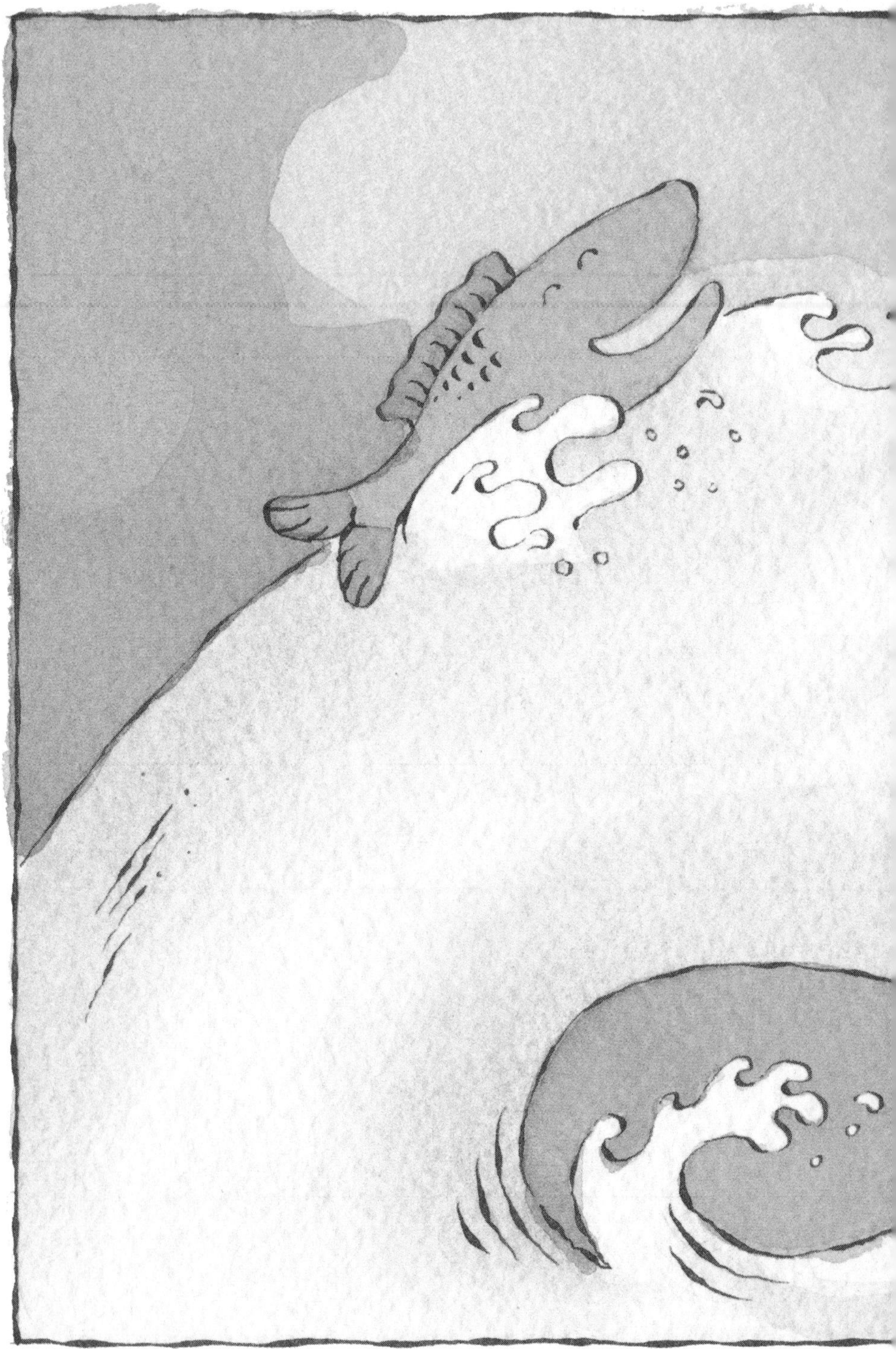

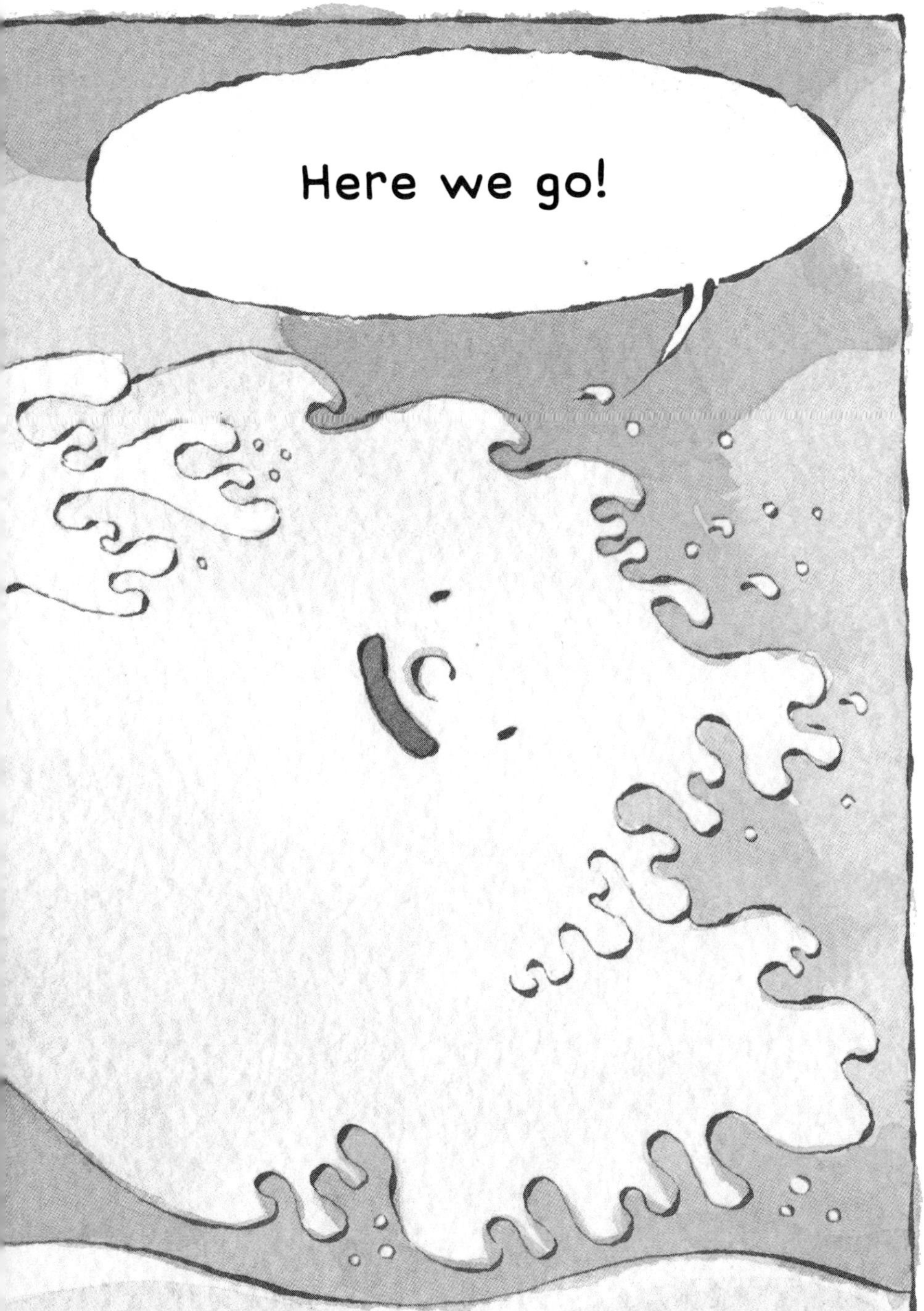
Here we go!

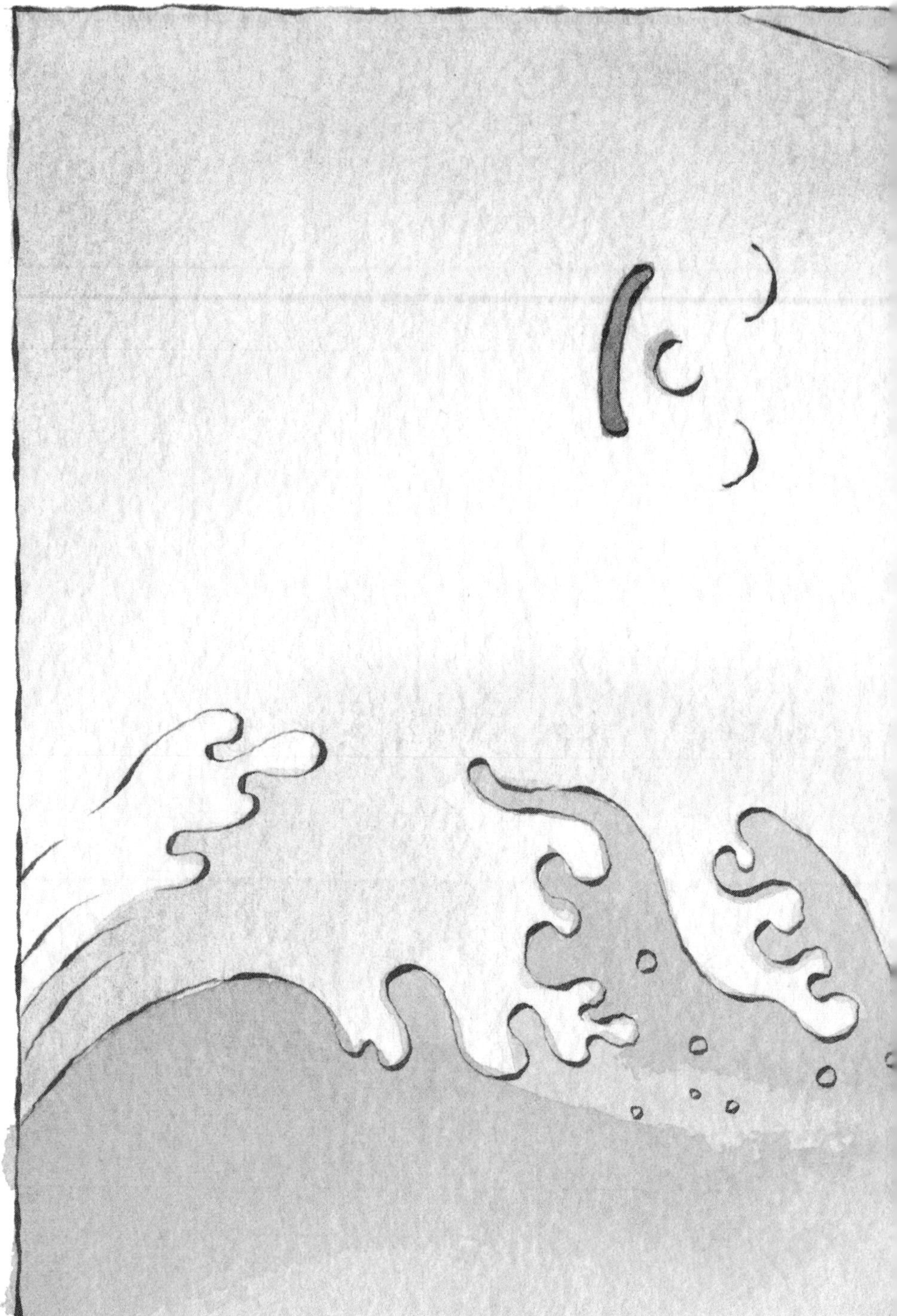

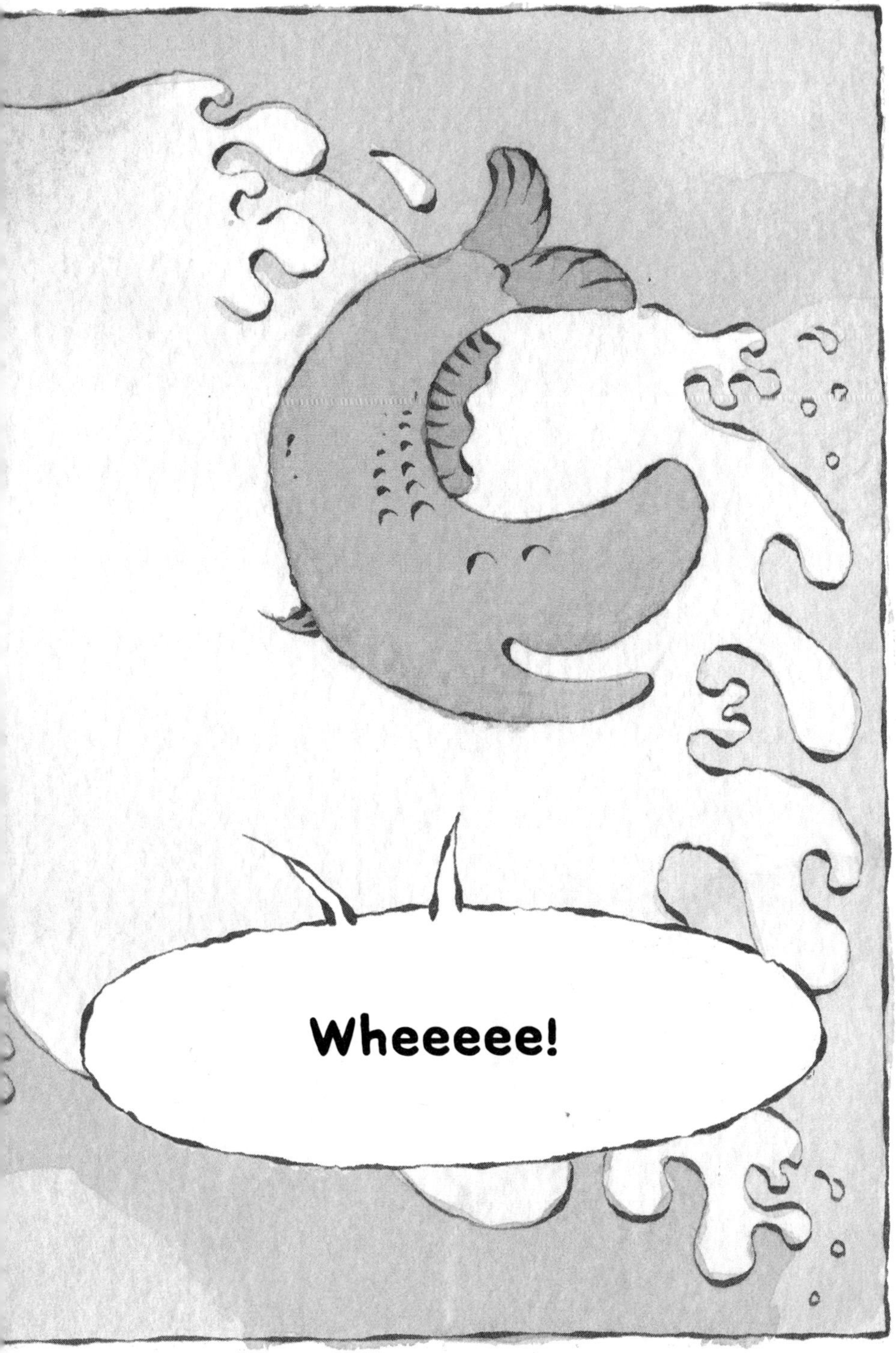
Wheeeee!

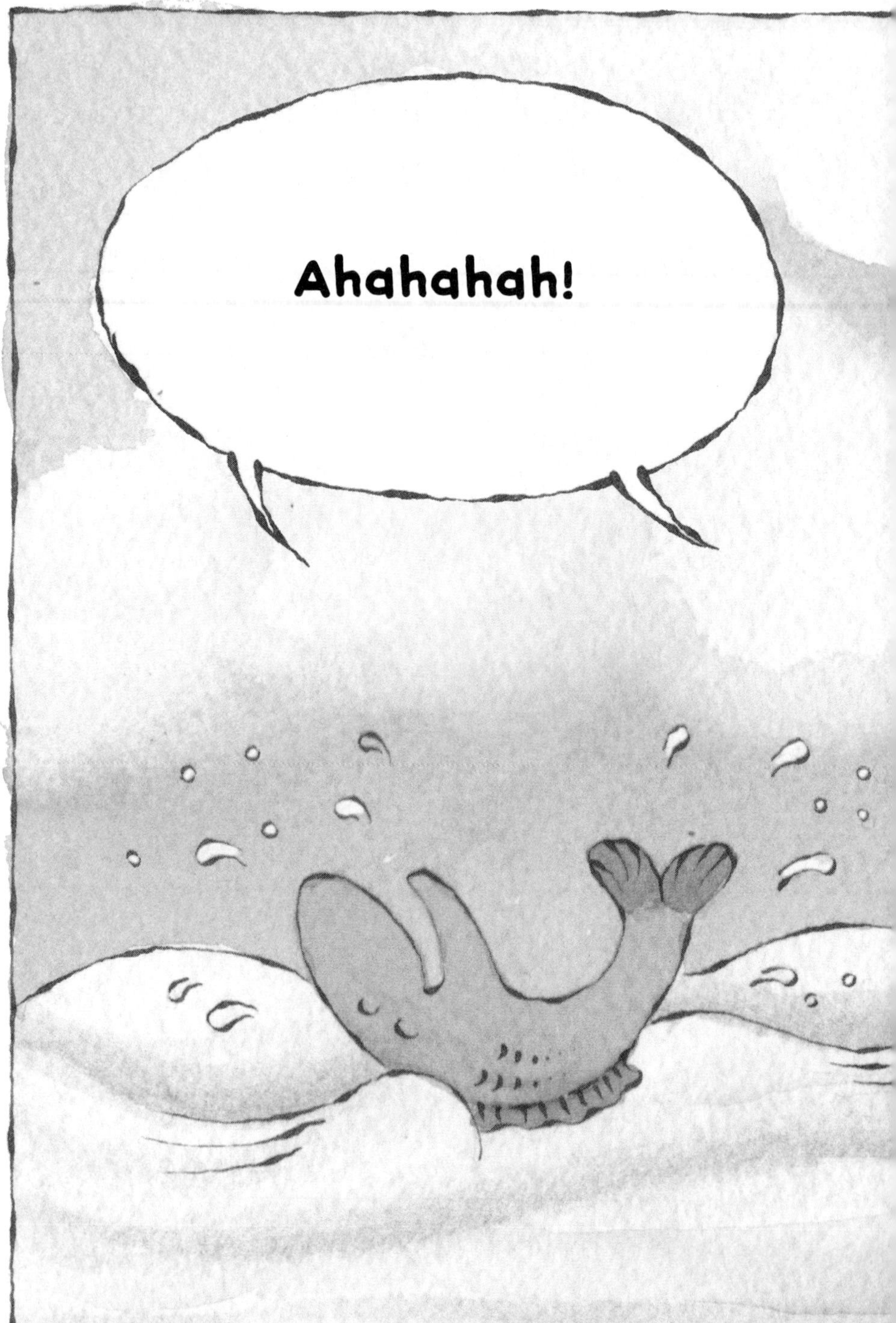
Ahahahah!

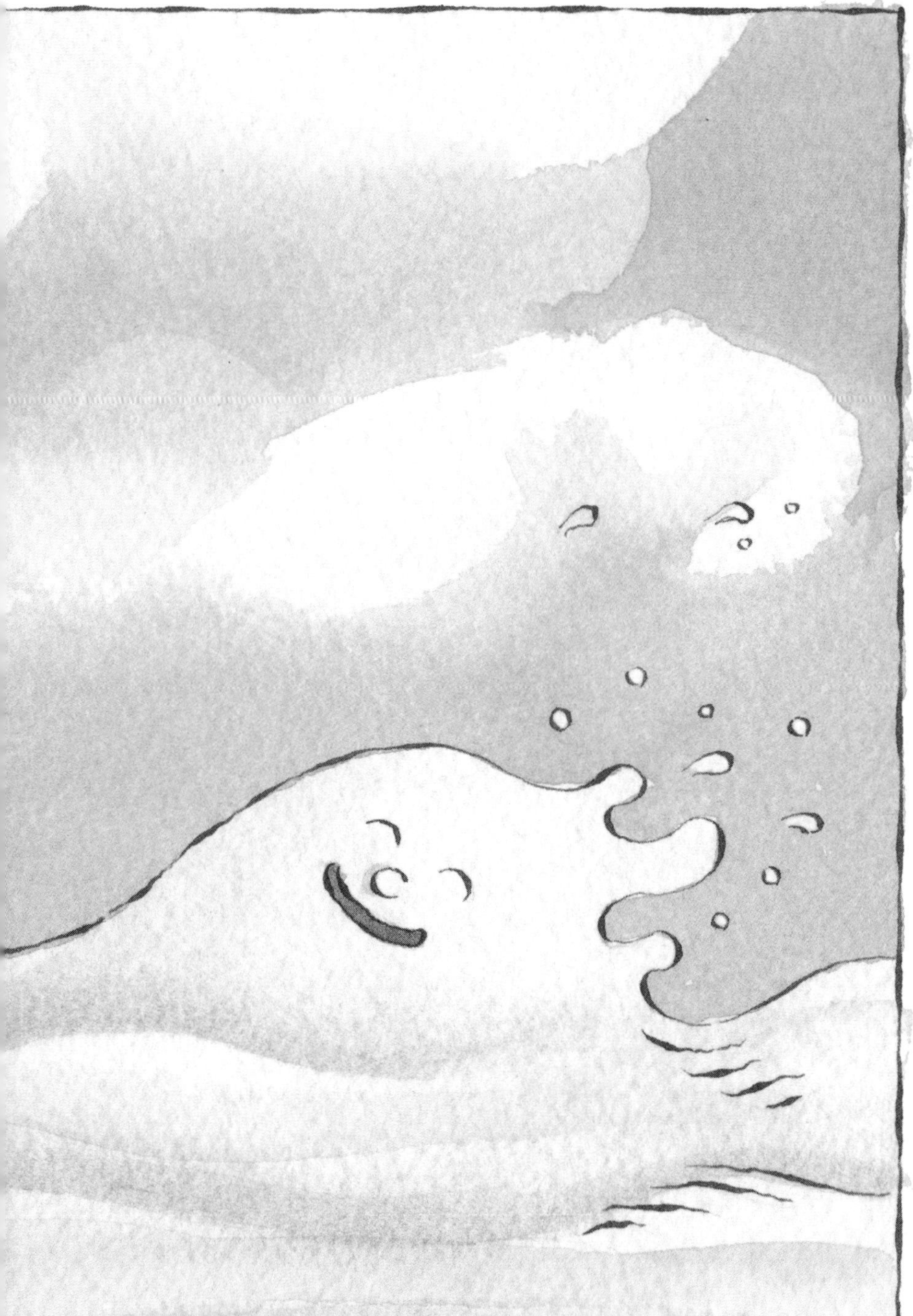

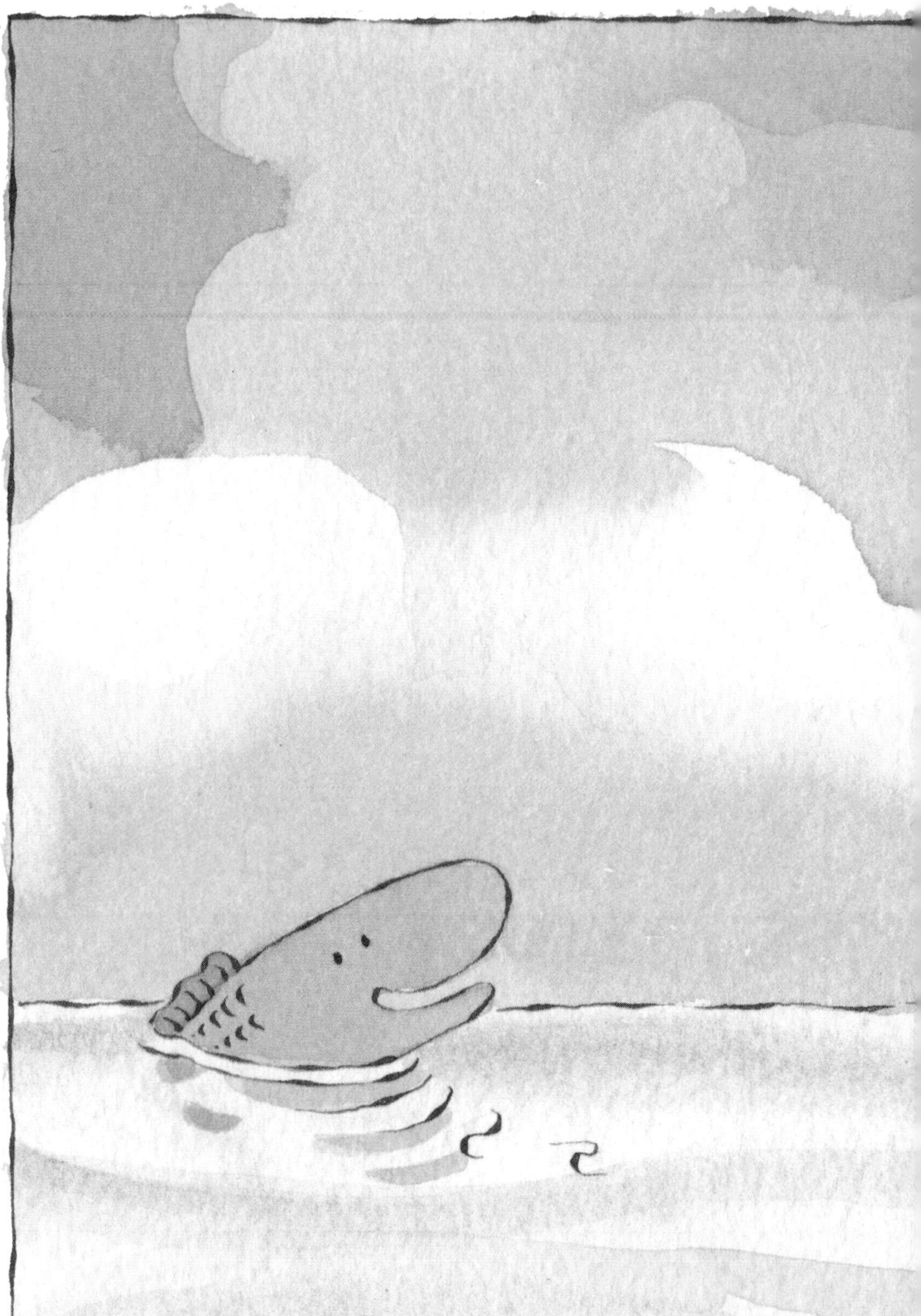

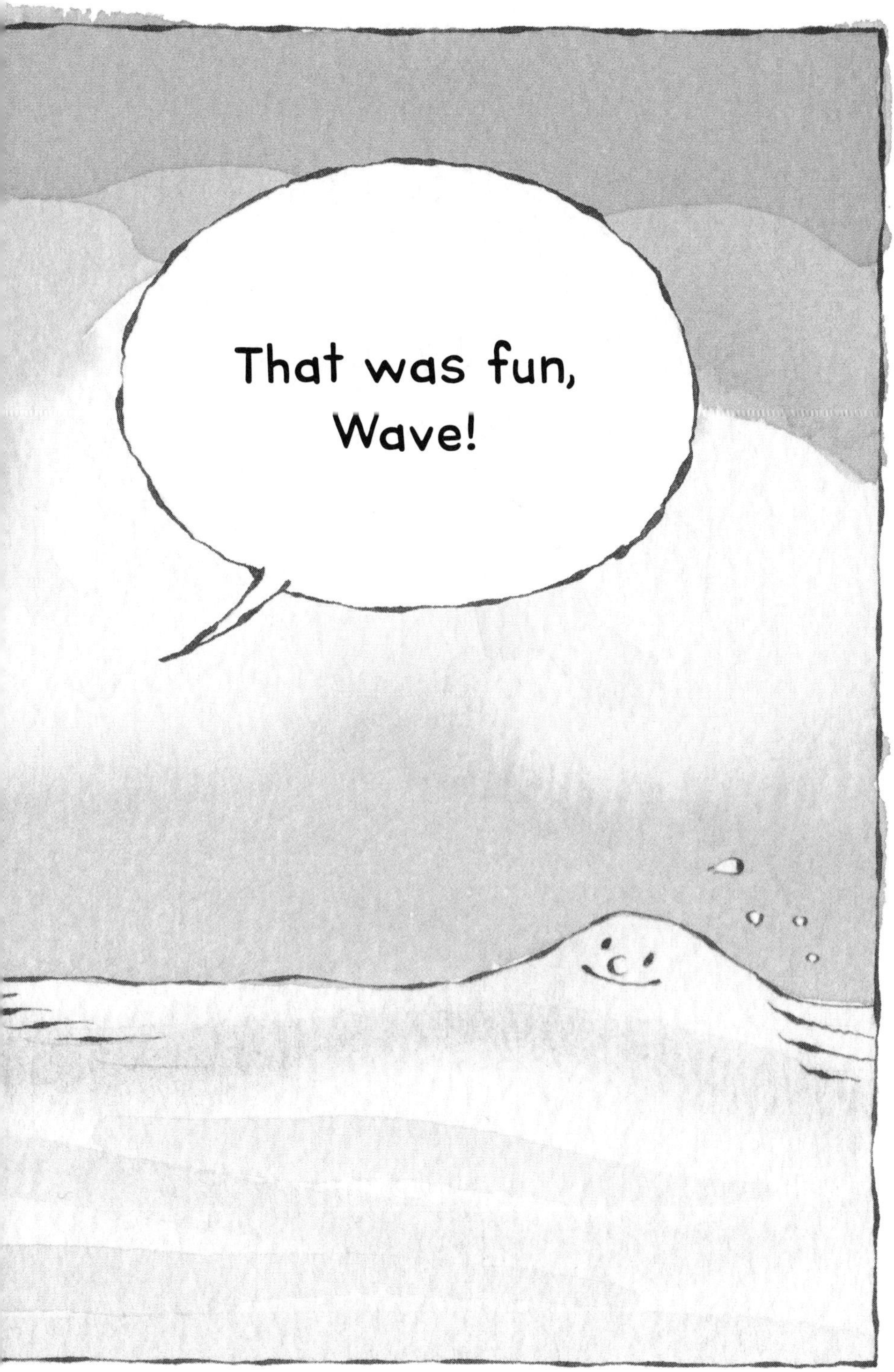
That was fun, Wave!

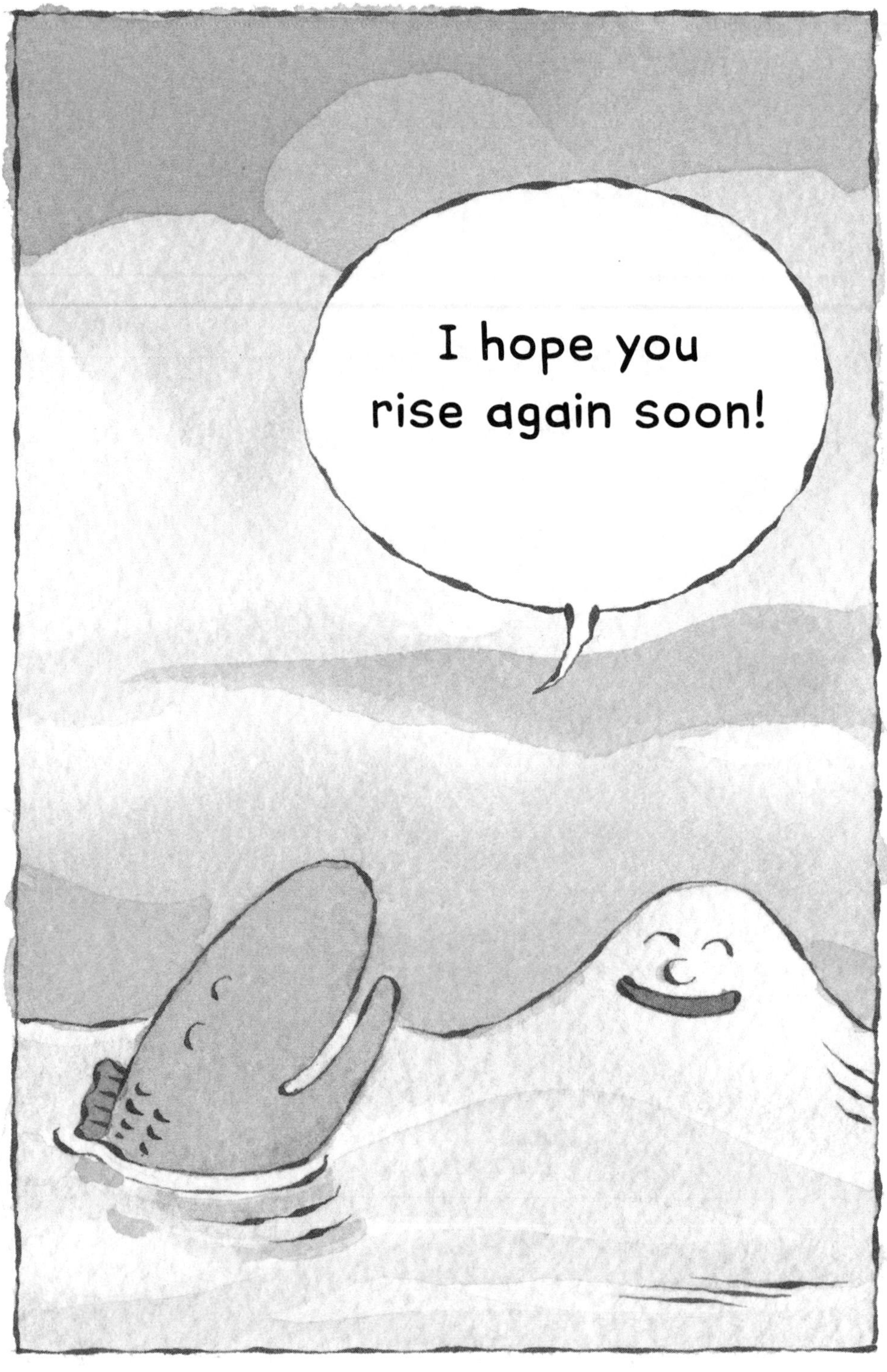
I hope you rise again soon!